"Vivian," Alec said, taking a step forward, and his voice vibrated on her name, "look at me."

Almost fearfully Vivian obeyed, raising her head until, nearly on a level with his, their eyes met and he held her glance almost, it seemed, against her will.

There was something inscrutable, something she half-feared, in his expression, and yet she had to look at him and she found herself murmuring almost inaudibly:

"What do you want me to do?"

She trembled when she had spoken, and then gravely his voice, just barely audible to her hearing, answered:

"I want you to learn to love me."

Also in Pyramid Books
by
BARBARA CARTLAND

DESIRE OF THE HEART
A HAZARD OF HEARTS
THE COIN OF LOVE
LOVE IN HIDING
THE ENCHANTING EVIL
THE UNPREDICTABLE BRIDE
THE SECRET HEART
A DUEL OF HEARTS
LOVE IS THE ENEMY
THE HIDDEN HEART
LOST ENCHANTMENT
LOVE HOLDS THE CARDS
LOST LOVE
LOVE ME FOREVER
LOVE IS CONTRABAND
THE INNOCENT HEIRESS
LOVE IS DANGEROUS
THE AUDACIOUS
   ADVENTURESS
THE ENCHANTED MOMENT
SWEET ADVENTURE
THE ROYAL PLEDGE
WINGS ON MY HEART
WE DANCED ALL NIGHT
THE COMPLACENT WIFE
A HALO FOR THE DEVIL
LOVE IS AN EAGLE
THE LITTLE PRETENDER
THE GOLDEN GONDOLA
STARS IN MY HEART
MESSENGER OF LOVE
THE SECRET FEAR
AN INNOCENT IN PARIS
METTERNICH, THE
   PASSIONATE DIPLOMAT
WHERE IS LOVE?
TOWARDS THE STARS
AN INNOCENT IN MAYFAIR

THE WINGS OF LOVE
THE ENCHANTED WALTZ
THE HIDDEN EVIL
ELIZABETHAN LOVER
THE UNKNOWN HEART
OPEN WINGS
AGAIN THIS RAPTURE
THE RELUCTANT BRIDE
THE PRETTY HORSE-BREAKERS
THE KISS OF THE DEVIL
A KISS OF SILK
NO HEART IS FREE
LOVE TO THE RESCUE
STOLEN HALO
SWEET PUNISHMENT
LIGHTS OF LOVE
BLUE HEATHER
THE IRRESTIBLE BUCK
OUT OF REACH
THE SCANDALOUS LIFE
   OF KING CAROL
THE THIEF OF LOVE
WOMAN, THE ENIGMA
ARMOUR AGAINST LOVE
JOSEPHINE, EMPRESS
   OF FRANCE
THE PASSIONATE PILGRIM
THE BITTER WINDS OF
   LOVE
THE DREAM WITHIN
THE MAGIC OF HONEY
A HEART IS BROKEN
THEFT OF A HEART
ELIZABETH, EMPRESS
   OF AUSTRIA
AGAINST THE STREAM
LOVE AND LINDA

DESPERATE DEFIANCE

Barbara Cartland

PYRAMID BOOKS   NEW YORK

Pyramid Books are published by Pyramid Publications (Har-
court Brace Jovanovich). Its trademarks, consisting of the word
"Pyramid" and the portrayal of a pyramid, are registered in the
United States Patent Office.

PYRAMID PUBLICATIONS
(Harcourt Brace Jovanovich)
757 Third Avenue, New York, N.Y. 10017

AUTHOR'S NOTE

This book, written in 1936, portrays accurately the position of Tibet at that time in relation to other countries.

Also, the difference between the Laws of the Red Hats and the Yellow Hats and the description of the country and people of Tibet is as authentic as many years of research can make it.

CHAPTER ONE
1936

Vivian Carrow rested her elbows on the table and looked at the fashionable throng chattering, laughing, and drinking around her.

From inside the Casino came the sounds of a band and the murmur of many voices as the crowds sauntered in and out of the gambling rooms.

Women, beautifully dressed, their diamonds flashing, and glittering, protested loudly that they were 'completely broke.'

The genuine spendthrifts hurried by, clutching their worn system cards in their hands, giving hardly a glance to the glamorous gaiety outside on the terrace.

Men and women, representative of Society in every country in Europe, rubbed shoulders with the cocottes of every race.

The *habitués*, who belonged to no nation but lived year after year in Monte Carlo, eked out a precarious existence as they gambled daily on the green-baize tables.

To Vivian, it was all new, amusing, and exciting.

Her life had never brought her in contact with this colorful, superficial, and sophisticated life which she found now surging round her like a kaleidoscope.

Among ordinary people Vivian stood out not only as a pretty girl, but with something more arresting in her face than mere looks.

There was character in the dark grey eyes, set rather wide apart under straight, firmly marked eyebrows.

There was determination in the set of her small round chin which completed the perfect oval of her face, framed by dark hair with a glint of bronze in its curly waves.

Her mouth was firm and held a promise of deep emotions not yet awakened to maturity.

Vivian's party was quiet and unspectacular.

Her aunt, Lady Dalton, sat at the head of the table, her hair streaked with grey, her pearls small but perfect, her dress obviously suitable for a woman who was nearing sixty.

She was in striking contrast to the hostess at the next table, whose hands and neck starkly proclaimed her age, while her face masked by cosmetics, revealed rather than concealed the ravages of years.

Withered shoulders peeped, naked from a dress of soft pink chiffon which might have become a young girl.

A necklace of diamonds, a huge sheaf of exotic orchids could not hide the obvious pathos of a woman striving to defeat Time.

Vivian watched this woman, and gradually her red mouth curled a little in contempt at the fawning attentions of the two men who partnered the painted spectacle at supper.

Suave, dark, and tight-waisted, they were both old enough to be her sons, or young enough to have paid their attentions to her daughter, who was at that moment returning to the table.

The daughter was as flamboyant as the mother, but besides her jewels and orchids she had the priceless possession of youth.

It was not the daughter who Vivian watched as she returned to the table, but the man who escorted her.

Tall, good-looking, with that indefinable air of good breeding, he seemed curiously out of place amid the vulgarity of people with whom he was supping.

He held the chair back for his partner to sit down and then drew his own chair to the table and lifted a glass of champagne to his lips.

As he did so he looked across at Vivian and smiled.

Their eyes met and she smiled back at him, her whole face lighting up as if with some inner radiance.

8

Just for a moment their eyes held each others', and then they both turned to their neighbors with a conventional commonplace remark.

Vivian's pensive mood had gone.

She drew the retired Rear-Admiral who sat on her left into conversation, and her sparkling and spontaneous interest soon set him talking about his life in the 'good old days.'

He was too engrossed in the sound of his own voice to realize that after the first moment or two she was not listening to what he was saying.

"How I love Jimmy!" Vivian was whispering to herself. "How glad I am that I came here. If only we were in the same party."

Vivian was twenty-three, and yet this was the first time she had ever come to the fashionable South of France in the summer season.

Every other year she had spent the late summer and autumn either travelling in strange countries with her father, seeing new lands, or else at home.

This was in a quiet little Worcestershire village, studying in preparation for the next exploration, or filing, writing, and indexing the information her father had acquired in the previous months.

Ever since she was fourteen, when her mother had died, Vivian had been Professor Carrow's constant companion wherever he went.

He was the greatest authority on mineralogy in England, possibly in the world, and he was also what Vivian had called, ever since she was tiny, a 'maker of maps.'

Wherever there was uncharted land, Professor Carrow would be sent, and sooner or later his findings would be adopted by the Geographical Society to be incorporated later in the atlas.

It was a strange life for a girl, but Vivian adored it and had asked for nothing better, until just three months ago.

Then she met Jimmy Loring.

They had been introduced casually but conventionally at her father's club in Pall Mall.

"Such a strange place to meet an attractive young man," Vivian had thought afterwards.

He had been lunching with his uncle and she with her father. The old men had been talking when she arrived, a little late and flustered because her shopping had kept her until past the appointed luncheon hour.

"I cannot apologize enough, Daddy dear," she had said, hurrying into the somewhat lugubrious waiting-room where the sexes were allowed to intermingle.

Then she found herself introduced to General Loring and to his nephew.

Even as Jimmy took her hand and she raised her eyes to meet his she felt something strange was happening to her.

They all lunched together, but afterwards Vivian could never remember what they had talked about.

She was only conscious of feeling absurdly happy, of being unusually amused, and of finding that it was three o'clock almost before she realized they had started their meal.

"Three o'clock! It can't be true!" she said ruefully, as the clock on the mantelpiece struck the hour. "I had an appointment at a quarter to three."

"Let me drive you there," Jimmy Loring had suggested.

"Would you really?" Vivian said. Then she hesitated. "But it may be out of your way. I want to go to Harrods."

"I would love to take you," he protested.

The Professor had nodded his approval from the head of the table.

"Don't wait for us, my dear," he said. "It is not often I meet an old friend, and we shall sit here over our port for at least another half-hour."

Outside the Club, Jimmy's tiny sports car had awaited them.

He had offered to close the hood in case it should be too windy for her, but Vivian had pooh-poohed the idea.

"I am used to the wind," she had answered. "My father and I have just come back from the north of Canada, and London seems absolutely stifling."

Somehow they never found their way to Harrods that afternoon. They had driven round the park, they had sat watching the Serpentine glimmer in the spring sunshine.

They had talked of themselves, of life, of hopes, and again of themselves, until finally the pale sun was sinking behind Kensington Palace.

"I will call for you at nine o'clock," Jimmy had said when eventually he dropped her at the quiet, unpretentious hotel at which she and her father were staying.

Vivian had run upstairs with burning cheeks and a thumping heart.

"I love him," she had said to herself unashamedly in the privacy of her own bedroom.

"I love you!" she whispered to Jimmy two nights later, when he kissed her for the first time.

The summer had passed in a golden haze, leaving a panorama of memories—long days spent drifting down the river Avon in a cushioned punt, or afternoons exploring the neighborhood of the black and white sixteenth-century house which, to the Professor and Vivian, was the most perfect spot on earth.

The Manor House was a pretentious name for their house.

The rooms were small and few so that more than two guests seemed a crowd, but for the Professor it fulfilled all his requirements.

To Vivian who had known and loved every inch of the estate since she was a baby, it meant home in the fullest and deepest sense of the word.

"Has anyone ever been so happy before?" she asked Jimmy, as they sat on the river bank listening to the soft whispering of the summer breeze through the rushes.

"I think that someone might have made that remark before," Jimmy teased.

"Don't laugh at me," Vivian said solemnly. "Answer me."

He turned round to face her, and putting out his hand raised her face to his.

"Never," he replied seriously. "It is impossible that anyone could ever be as happy as we are."

"Really truly?" Vivian asked.

"Really truly," Jimmy repeated, and kissed her.

Six weeks of delirious joy, and then had come a moment of parting, when Jimmy had to go to London to take up a job in an insurance office.

"My uncle has fixed it," he told Vivian. "That is why I was lunching with him that day."

She slipped her hand into his.

"I will come down every weekend," he promised, "but I have got to work very hard, my darling, and if you can't guess the reason why, I shan't tell you."

Of course she could guess the reason and of course she thought of little else.

Marriage with Jimmy, having him all to herself, a tiny home together, was all she dreamt of, all she thought about in the weeks that followed.

Then Jimmy announced that he had been invited to Monte Carlo.

"They are extraordinary people," he had confessed to Vivian. "Stubbs is their name. They are enormously rich, and they might be useful, one never knows. I shall have to go, darling, but can't you come too? You must know somebody who would put you up."

"There is Father's sister," Vivian had said reflectively. "My Aunt Geraldine. She has a villa there, and she has often asked me to go and stay but I have always refused."

"But that is marvelous!" Jimmy said enthusiastically. "Write to her at once. It is all too perfect. You will adore it. Monte Carlo is the most enjoyable place in the world."

"I have always hated the idea of it," Vivian confessed. "Crowds of smart people with wonderful clothes is not my idea of fun."

"Nonsense!" Jimmy had replied. "You will love it."

"I shall be terrified of them," Vivian said.

"With me to look after you?" Jimmy asked. "What a little goose you are! Sit down and write at once."

So Vivian had obeyed and had received from her aunt a letter of welcome and affection.

It was all just as she had imagined it would be, Vivian thought on arrival.

The blue sky and sea, the practically naked bodies sunbathing on expensive mattresses, lacquered toe-nails, oiled backs, diamond cigarette-cases, luxurious cars, the calm efficiency of 'the tables.'

Tonight, as she sat at supper, Vivian could see the spotlights being fixed ready to illuminate the floating stage on which a monster cabaret costing thousands of francs would shortly commence.

Above them in the sky there were stars while floodlights on the old casino made it look like a white-iced cake.

The shrill, discordant laugh of Mrs. Stubbs echoed from the neighboring table and startled Vivian from her reverie.

"How I dislike that woman!" she thought, and in the wake of that dislike came a sudden nausea.

"Is anything the matter?" the Admiral asked her anxiously.

"I am quite all right," she said, reassuring herself as much as him. "A moment's giddiness, that is all. Surely it is very hot tonight?"

"The place is like an oven," the Admiral replied. "But you have no right to complain. Look at the uncomfortable clothes we poor men have to wear."

Vivian laughingly agreed, wondering how often she had heard that remark.

"Let us go up on to the roof and dance. It may be cooler there," her partner suggested.

"Yes, let us go there," Vivian said, glad of an excuse to move.

They rose to their feet, threading their way through the tables.

"Don't be long, darling," Lady Dalton said to Vivian. "The cabaret will start in another ten minutes."

"We will be back by then," Vivian answered her, and turned towards the doorway.

In the crowded vestibule which led to the roof garden and to the gambling rooms, the Admiral stopped to speak to some friends of his. As she waited, Vivian felt a hand on her arm.

She knew without turning her head.

"Darling," she whispered beneath her breath.

"I have to see you," Jimmy said.

"You can't want to more than I do," Vivian replied. "Oh, Jimmy, I have seen practically nothing of you the last three days."

"I know," he said. "When can I see you, Vivian? It is important."

"Darling," she replied, "any time, anywhere. You know that is all I am here for."

"I will come to the garden of the villa in about two hours' time," he said.

"The garden of the villa?" Vivian echoed almost stupidly.

"Yes," he answered. "Wait for me by the little summer house. I won't be later than I can help."

Without waiting for her answer, he disappeared as quickly as he had come, elbowing his way through the crowds to the terrace again.

Vivian stood looking after him and then she felt wildly happy.

She had not really enjoyed this past week. She had seen Jimmy every day but generally for only a few fleeting seconds, or with a crowd of people round them.

They had met at the bathing pool, on the tennis courts, or aboard one of the many small yachts which steamed out of the harbor for an afternoon's amusement.

It had all been gay and amusing and what Jimmy's friends called 'fun,' but it was not Vivian's idea of real enjoyment and happiness.

Jimmy to herself, Jimmy in the garden beside the Avon, was what she wanted.

From the moment she had stepped on to Monte Carlo station a week ago she had been fêted, entertained, and amused but denied the only thing which could make her happy.

Now he wanted her and he was coming to see her alone tonight in the quietness and peace of the villa garden.

Vivian gave a little shiver of excitement.

"I have to see you," Jimmy had said.

CHAPTER TWO

"There is the most dangerous man in Europe," said the Admiral as they moved slowly round to a dreamy tune crooned by a blonde.

"Where?" Vivian asked, her dreams of Jimmy interrupted.

"You see that Indian standing by the pillar, talking to a fat American women covered in emeralds?"

"Oh, yes, I see him," Vivian replied. "Who is he?"

"That is Dhilangi," the Admiral answered.

"But of course I have heard of him," Vivian said. "He is another Gandhi or something, isn't he?"

"Far worse," her partner said. "And what is more, my dear, you are seeing history in the making."

"Why?" Vivian asked.

"Well, the woman in emeralds," the Admiral answered, "is Mrs. Michael Mackie, widow of the oil king from America."

"But why history?" Vivian asked. "Is she going to finance him or something?"

"That is just the question, my dear young lady," her partner said, "that at least a quarter of the world is asking at this precise moment."

"Why, what would happen if she does?" Vivian questioned.

"God knows what will not happen!" the Admiral

answered ruefully. "Dhilangi is one of the most dangerous people we have ever had to deal with in India. He is entirely unscrupulous, completely self-seeking, and at the same time carried away by a fanaticism and fire.

"Wherever he goes there is insurrection and rebellion. He has already cost us many lives and a great deal of worry, but up till now he has been handicapped by lack of money.

"Unlike Gandhi, he is by no means an ascetic. He likes luxury, he likes comfort, and he wants all the things that money can buy.

"If he can persuade Mrs. Mackie to finance or marry him, (I believe he is prepared to go to such lengths), the situation will be very serious indeed."

"Is she so tremendously rich?" Vivian asked.

"Fabulously," the Admiral answered. "And what is more to the point is that she thinks this man a kind of new Messiah and fancies herself as his inspiration."

"It all sounds to me rather like a sensational story in the newspapers," Vivian said. "Are you really being serious?"

"There is no joke about it, I assure you," the Admiral replied. "The powers that be have done everything they can to prevent such an alliance taking place, but what can they do in this so-called civilized world when we all insist on the freedom of the individual."

"And is she to decide now—I mean here at Monte Carlo—is that why they are together?" Vivian asked.

"So we understand," answered the Admiral. "There is no doubt that Dhilangi travelled here especially to meet the lady in question."

As they moved slowly past on the crowded dance floor, Vivian looked at the Indian with interest. He was thin and short and there were all the signs of dissipation in his face.

But she could see that there was also, an eager, almost super-normal, vitality about him.

There was also something savage and untamed in the gesture of his hand and the movements of his thin lips.

"He is like a tiger waiting to spring," Vivian said after watching him for a moment, and then laughed apologetically. "That sounds very banal, and yet I can't help it. That is what he reminds me of."

"It is a very apt simile," her partner said shortly.

As they neared the door he steered her skilfully towards it and they made their way downstairs.

"Will the time never pass?" Vivian wondered to herself.

It seemed to her that a century must tick by before she could get home and wait for Jimmy to come to her.

The cabaret with its immense chorus of semi-naked women wearing half a million francs' worth of ostrich feathers failed to amuse her.

The glittering finale of naked legs, and top hats made of looking-glass, passed unnoticed by her as she tried to catch a glimpse of Jimmy, who had moved to the other end of the terrace with his noisy and raffish party.

"How awful for him to have to stay with such people," Vivian thought.

Tales of how Mrs. Stubbs had taken a whole floor at the Beach Hotel for herself and her guests, of her three Hispano-Suiza cars decorated in chocolate brown and driven by black chauffeurs, were the talk of everyone in Monte Carlo.

"But *who* are the Stubbs?" a newcomer would ask—to be answered by a chorus of, "You can't tub without Stubbs."

Everyone had seen the advertisements in England of the new washing powder which was, as Jimmy said, guaranteed to do everything in the world except drive a motorcar.

Out of his patent mixture, with the help of tremendous advertising, Mr. Stubbs had accumulated a fortune in a short number of years.

"If Jimmy gets his insurance, perhaps we shall be able to get married," Vivian thought.

At last, as the clock struck one, Lady Dalton rose.

Only Vivian and her aunt descended at the villa high on the Corniche road overlooking the sea, the car taking on the rest of the guests to the hotels and villas at which they were staying.

"I have enjoyed myself. Thank you so much, Aunt Geráldine," Vivian said.

"I am afraid we were rather an old party for you," her aunt replied. "But though I live here I seldom go to the galas at the Casino and all my friends are rather ancient and staid, I am afraid."

"Nonsense!" Vivian replied, laughing. "The Admiral was as chirpy as a two-year-old, and I think he enjoyed dancing."

"I am quite sure he did with you," her aunt replied. "But whether you enjoyed yourself is another matter."

"Well, I promise you I did," Vivian answered, kissing her again and going into her bedroom.

She waited a moment until her aunt's door was firmly shut and then, turning out the light, she tip-toed softly down the carpeted stairs.

She cautiously opened the french window into the garden and walked out.

The garden was not very wide, and marched beside that of the villa next door; but it wended its way downhill by a series of little paths until it came to a lower road, beyond which was the sea.

Here there was a small summerhouse with roses climbing over it and the sweet perfume of night-scented stock.

All was very quiet and still. Out to sea a lighthouse flashed intermittently.

There were the little lights of Cap Gerrat and the twinkle of the stars overhead.

Vivian felt that she was part of the mystery and beauty of it all.

The noise of an approaching car made her start and look anxiously over the high wall into the roadway, but it stopped at a gate further down and her heart started beating again.

It was not Jimmy.

There was a sound of voices and laughter, and she realized that the people of the next door villa had come home.

Curiosity made her move away from the summerhouse and peep through the dividing hedge into the garden of the Villa Sebastian.

She could see several people descending from a large Rolls Royce.

Watching them, Vivian saw a vivacious American—who was talking at the top of her voice—gesticulating so that her diamond bracelets glittered and flashed in the light of the car's headlamps.

18

With her were several men, all more or less the worse for drink, and two others—Mrs. Mackie and Dhilangi.

"So they are staying next door," Vivian thought. "How amusing! Perhaps he will propose to her in the garden and I shall know the answer to the problem which is worrying Europe."

She heard Mrs. Mackie say to the chauffeur,

"Wait here for Mr. Dhilangi."

Then, talking and laughing the whole party moved up the garden towards the villa.

Slowly Vivian retraced her steps to the summerhouse. She was waiting more impatiently for Jimmy now.

Somehow the calm beauty of the night had been broken by the noise and chatter of the party next door.

She could no longer feel the beauty of sea and sky enveloping her. She could only wait, every nerve alert for the sound of another car.

At last she heard one coming. She held her breath and prayed it might be Jimmy and that the headlights would not sweep by.

Then, just when she thought she was to be disappointed again there was the sound of brakes and a few seconds later she heard Jimmy's footsteps coming towards her.

She sat still, savoring the moment, almost afraid to break the silence which seemed to hold her, bound and palpitating, in the shadow of the little summerhouse.

The next moment he was beside her.

"Jimmy," she said, and put out her arms.

He held her stiffly and did not kiss her.

"Darling," she said. "I thought you were never coming."

Then his attitude and his silence stuck her as strange.

"What is it?" she asked apprehensively. "What is the matter?"

He moved a few paces away from her and stood looking out towards the sea, his figure silhouetted against the sky.

She could see the outline of his head, the strong square-cut shoulders, and his height which always made her feel small and yet so comfortingly protected in his arms.

"Jimmy," she said again sharply. "What is it?"

He turned towards her and took both her hands in his. She could not see his features although she tried, she only knew that he was looking anxious and worried.

19

"Listen, Vivian," he said. "I have come here to tell you something, and now I don't know how to do it."

His voice was hard and unlike himself. Vivian felt a sudden chill of fear sweep over her.

"Tell me," she said. "You must tell me. Jimmy, what is it that you are afraid to tell me?"

There was a moment's silence and then, as if he made a tremendous effort, Jimmy spoke:

"I am going to marry Marjorie Stubbs."

Vivian stood absolutely still. They faced each other in the dim shadows.

"It isn't true," Vivian thought swiftly. "I am not hearing this. I ought to be screaming, crying, fainting with pain, or dying at his feet; but I am not. I am standing still and hearing it."

Nearly a minute must have passed and then, surprisingly clear and firm her voice said—

"Why?"

Only then did Jimmy release her hands. Again he turned his back on her and stared out to sea.

"Why do you think?" he said harshly, and as Vivian did not reply, he went on; "Because she has money, because I have got to have it. Don't you understand—don't you see, Vivian? I cannot live without it.

"I loathe the office, I loathe the hum-drum existence I have been living in London, pinching and saving, beastly lodgings, second rate food.

"And the eternal struggle to keep myself alive and decent. I can't stand it, I tell you—and this is the way out."

Vivian felt as if she were acting in some play. It was not she who stood there; it was not she, with dry eyes, who was listening to the man to whom she had given not only her heart but her soul.

"He does not want me," she thought. "This is the end."

It seemed so incredible, so unreal, that she almost laughed out loud; and yet she knew that he was gone. Already the Jimmy she had known had left her.

Again there was a long silence, and then Jimmy spoke.

"I am sorry, Vivian. Speak to me," he said a moment later. "Say something. Reproach me, curse me, but don't keep silent. If only you knew how I hate myself for doing this. How I loathe and despise myself for the way I am behaving—and yet I cannot help it, Vivian."

As if her very silence had exasperated him beyond endurance, he put his arms round her, drew her close to him, and kissed her cheek and then her mouth.

He might have been kissing a dead woman. She made neither response nor repulsion, and she felt nothing.

It was unlike any kiss she had ever had from Jimmy because nothing within her responded.

She was still acting, still outside this amazing scene, watching it—a stranger watching a stranger's emotions.

Almost roughly Jimmy took his arms away from her. He was becoming embarrassed by her silence. It was not what he expected and he did not understand it.

He stood for a moment staring at her in the darkness as if striving to read her expression.

Then, unable to bear it any longer, the whole thing too much for him, he turned and left her, finding his way down the cliff gravel path and down the stone steps.

There was the sharp bang of a car door, the noise of the engine starting up, and Vivian was alone.

Slowly, almost deliberately, she sat down on the little wooden seat which ran along the inside wall of the summerhouse.

Slowly her fingers interlaced, her nails biting deeply into the flesh, but she had no knowledge of the pain she was causing herself.

She stared with wide eyes straight in front of her. Her lips tried to form Jimmy's name, and then one by one bitter tears began to course down her cheeks.

Suddenly there was the sound of a car coming up the road, and the noise of it galvanized her into sudden aliveness.

Vivian jumped to her feet and stood quivering and listening.

Nearer and nearer came the hum of the engine until with a flicker of lights it had passed.

Only when the last sound of it had died away into the distance did Vivian fling out her arms in a despairing gesture and call Jimmy's name.

Her voice broke on the word, and as if it had snapped her control, her whole body was shaken a moment later by uncontrollable sobs.

The storm of weeping made her bury her face in her

hands, the tears trickling through her fingers; her knees seemed to give under her.

Blindly groping her way she sank, half sitting, half lying down on the wooden seat.

"It isn't true, it isn't true! Jimmy, my own Jimmy!" she repeated again and again.

Her voice was choked and the only sound was her sobbing breath.

The garden was very quiet. There was no wind, and the trees and flowers, dimly under the stars, seemed to stand sentinel before the death of a love which could never blossom again.

Suddenly the silence was broken by a sharp report, the noise of a motor backfiring or of a gunshot.

Vaguely Vivian heard it, and the mere effort of listening checked the wildness of her tears.

She raised herself from the rough, unpolished wood. In an effort for breath she threw back her head, and as she did so she stiffened.

A man had come swiftly toward the summerhouse and was standing just outside. He was not very tall and she could see that he was wearing evening clothes, his white shirt and cuffs visible in the surrounding dusk.

She tried to say, "What do you want?"

But her voice was too choked, and the only result of her effort was an inarticulate sound, almost a groan.

Swiftly he stepped in toward her and she felt a thrill of fear; then his voice, low, cultured, and speaking English, somehow reassured her.

"Who is there?" he asked.

For a second she was incapable of answering. Then he drew something from his pocket, struck a match, and a tiny yellow flame flickered in his cupped hands.

"Don't look at me," Vivian said sharply, instinctively.

She dropped her swollen eyes before the flickering illumination and then they were in the darkness again.

"Listen, Miss Carrow," the stranger said, speaking quietly. "I want you to help me."

"You know my name," Vivian said in surprise. "Who are you?"

"Never mind," came the low answer. "Listen to me. It is a question of moments. I know who you are, and I know you are used to standing by your father in difficult

22

situations. Do what I tell you now and you will be doing a great service to your country."

"But what?" Vivian tried to say.

The stranger however, took no notice of her interruptions.

"In a few seconds," he went on, speaking so low that she could hardly hear his voice, "a man or perhaps men will come here. Let them think we have been together for some time. You need not speak. I will do the talking. That is all I want you to do. Do you understand?"

"But why?" Vivian asked in a whisper.

"There's no time for questions," he replied stiffly.

A moment later she heard footsteps; and instantly with the sound, the stranger put his hand on hers, holding it tightly with firm, strong fingers.

She had no time to think, no time to consider her action, before two men stood outside the summerhouse and a torch was flashed on her face.

She gave an involuntary exclamation, the light was so unexpected, and she put her free hand to her eyes to shield them.

"What is it?" her unknown companion asked. "What are you doing here?"

"Pardon, *Monsieur*," came the answer in French, "but have you seen anyone pass through this garden?"

"Pass through the garden?" repeated Vivian's companion. He stood up and the light was directed on his face, but he had stepped forward a pace or so and as she had not moved she could see nothing but his back.

He had relinquished her hand as he moved, but not before the torch, like a sharp eye, had noted the movement.

"No one has gone through here so far as I know. What right have you to ask?"

"We are the police, *Monsieur*," came the reply.

"I am sorry," the Englishman said, "I am afraid I can't help you. Is anything the matter?"

"It is nothing," the gendarme answered. "A little trouble at the Villa next door."

"You yourself, *Monsieur*," interposed the other. "You have been here some time?"

"Oh, about twenty minutes. That is all. *Mademoiselle* and I were . . ." He hesitated for a second, then added, "just talking."

Again the torch flashed towards Vivian—played for a moment on her ravaged, tear-stained face, on her trembling hands holding a soaked white handkerchief. Then two hands went up to salute.

"*Milles pardonnes, Monsieur. Bon soir. Bon soir, Mademoiselle.*"

"Good night," replied the Englishman; and faintly Vivian answered, speaking for the first time.

"Good night."

Silently the two policemen disappeared in the direction from which they had come, through the fuchsia hedge and into the garden next door.

Vivian and her companion listened in silence, and then he turned towards her and said:

"Thank you, Miss Carrow. That was magnificent."

"What does it all mean?" she asked.

Instead of answering he put out his hand and drew her to her feet.

"I am going to take you back to the house," he said. "It is time you went to bed."

"Please tell me," she expostulated, "who you are. Why did you do this and why are you here?"

"Will you trust me?" he asked. "And believe that it was for a very good reason; and will you do one more thing for me—even if it is, maybe, the most difficult of all?"

"What is it?" she asked.

"Will you forget all about this tomorrow morning, and not repeat to anyone what has happened?"

She did not answer, and he added:

"Promise me, on your word of honor."

His voice was stern, almost commanding, and another time Vivian might have resented the rather authoritative note.

But she suddenly felt too exhausted and weary to argue. What did it matter—what did anything matter now?

"I promise," she answered.

Slowly and in silence they walked up the garden. At the foot of the steps which led up to the villa itself he paused.

"Good night, Miss Carrow," he said, holding out his hand. "Thank you again for what you have done and for your promise to say nothing."

Vivian put her hand in his.

"Good night," she said dully.

She felt the warmth and vitality glowing through his fingers.

"Don't be unhappy," he said. "Life is always an adventure, remember that."

And before she could answer he had turned and was striding away down the garden.

He walked on the grass rather than the path so that his departure was as silent as had been his arrival.

CHAPTER THREE

Vivian was going home by the Blue Train.

A week ago she had journeyed in it southwards, traveling joyfully towards her destination, knowing that every mile and every minute brought her nearer the man she loved.

Was she the same person, she asked herself, who had found it impossible to sleep because tomorrow had held such happiness that she could not bear to relinquish her thoughts of it?

Was she the same person who had welcomed the first sight of the blue sea and warm sun, not because they were beautiful but because they meant that in another hour she would be in Jimmy's arms?

She had not told her aunt why she wished to leave in such a hurry, but having seen her niece off at Nice station, Lady Dalton drove back to the Villa.

On the Upper Corniche road, she saw a long grey open tourer coming towards her.

In it as they swept past she recognized Jimmy and Marjorie Stubbs. Jimmy was bareheaded and his blue silk tennis shirt was open at the neck.

He was laughing, and he looked extraordinarily handsome as he skilfully rounded the bend and passed Lady Dalton.

Her face was very serious as she drove on. She was remembering Vivian's expression when she came downstairs that morning to announce her departure.

26

What had happened between these two eminently suited young people?

Puzzling over the problem she entered the Villa to find a huge box of pink roses lying on the hall table addressed to Vivian.

Perhaps these were a peace-offering, she thought hastily.

Perhaps the child had been too impetuous, rushing back to London without even trying to effect a reconciliation.

The thought of Jimmy's face as she had just seen him on the road made her hesitate doubtfully, and then slowly she slit open the little envelope which was tied to the flowers.

Inside was a plain visiting card such as is always supplied by florists, and on it were written two words in a strange, neat handwriting.

Thank you.

The problem was beyond Lady Dalton. She turned towards her sitting-room, taking the little card with her, which she intended to enclose in a letter to her niece.

She was stopped by Marie, the old cook who came towards her from the kitchen door obviously slightly agitated.

"What is it, Marie?" Lady Dalton asked.

"But Madame has not heard?" Marie replied, in the high, excited tones of a Frenchwoman who enjoys nothing more than a sensation whether tragedy or comedy.

"No, Marie," Lady Dalton said, smiling.

She was well used to Marie's excitements of one sort or another.

"I have heard nothing. What is it this time?"

"Madame has not heard of the tragedy next door, of what happened last night?" Marie inquired, delighted that she should be the first to bear the news.

"No, Marie; you must tell me," Lady Dalton said, leading the way into her sitting-room.

But it was not until the following day when she arrived in England that Vivian was to learn of what had occurred at the Villa Sebastian that night.

She stepped off the boat at Dover feeling tired and miserable. To her relief there was no one to meet her.

She had been afraid that her aunt might wire her father, and she was grateful that there were many hours more before she need face anyone she knew.

A little incident kept recurring to her mind as she lay with closed eyes in the deck cabin of the *Canterbury*.

Jimmy and she had been drifting downstream in a punt. He had bent over and kissed her as she lay back against the red cotton cushions.

"I wish we could drift on like this for ever," Vivian had said.

"You would get bored," Jimmy had replied.

"I should never get bored," Vivian had protested, and then suddenly her fingers had closed on his, holding them, almost desperately. "You won't get tired of me ever, will you, Jimmy? Promise me."

"Ridiculous one," Jimmy said, tipping her head back against his shoulder and bending to kiss her eyes.

"Why does love ever go?" Vivian asked later. "Why do people get tired and unhappy?"

"Because people don't love each other enough," Jimmy answered, and in his answer she had been content.

Yet now his reply haunted her. Had she not loved him enough?

And even while she tortured herself she knew that the truth lay in the fact that he had not loved her enough. How could money matter beside the true love of a man for a woman?

Money, money, money! The word seemed to haunt Vivian and almost roughly, she opened the newspaper that she had bought at Dover.

Idly she turned the pages over, striving to concentrate, to make the printed words hold her attention, and then headlines in the center page made her give a startled exclamation.

DEATH OF DHILANGI AT MONTE CARLO

The Monte Carlo police announce that Mr. Dhilangi, the well-known Indian agitator and revolutionary, was found in the garden of the Villa Sebastian in the early hours of Wednesday morning. A revolver was beside the body and everything seems to point to the suicide of this world famous figure.

Reasons for such an action are to be found in the fact that Mr. Dhilangi was known to have been seriously worried financially during the last few months.

The Casino authorities have stated that he had lost a small sum gambling that evening, and although friends have helped him, there is every reason to think that the strain of the unfortunate circumstances in which he found himself had told on his emotional and Oriental temperament. An inquest will be held this afternoon.

*　　*　　*　　*

Vivian read the paragraph through again, then her forehead knitted in an effort to concentrate. She was alone in the carriage and she drew down one of her big suit-cases from the rack where the porter had put it. She opened it.

It had been neatly and swiftly packed by Lady Dalton's maid, but she raised the layers of white tissue paper and quite near the top she found the white evening dress she had worn at the Casino the night before.

She drew it out of its folds and spread it open before her.

On the right-hand side of the skirt, just above the knee she found what she sought—a small mark where the stranger's knee had touched hers as they sat talking—a mark the colour of blood.

*　　*　　*　　*

As she entered the dining-room her father, seated at the breakfast-table, looked up with an affectionate smile.

Vivian pressed her cheek against his and then went to the sideboard where the silver dishes were kept warm on an electric plate.

"I am afraid I have eaten all the eggs," her father said.

"That's all right," Vivian replied. "I don't think I want anything."

She poured out her coffee and took her place at the table.

Her father followed her movements with an anxious look on his clever face.

As a mineralogist and cartographer of note, Professor Carrow was in demand by all sorts of people, and he found that his work led him into many queer and inter-esting places.

In the last few years he had refused those journeys on

which he could not take Vivian, and no amount of money or persuasion would make him change his mind.

It was a peculiar education for a young girl and not, perhaps, in some ways a particularly wise one.

But Vivian had managed to look after herself in strange circumstances; she had slept against a bag of concrete travelling up the Waikiki river; cooked an appetizing meal on the edge of the Sahara Desert, and made herself understood in strange dialects.

But she could always return to the Manor House for rest, peace and quiet happiness before setting out again on some strange adventure.

Then Jimmy Loring had come, disturbing and upsetting the peaceful little establishment. Dinner hours were altered, the guest room had to be renovated, the Professor's studies were interrupted by laughing, chattering voices.

But wise in his generation, Professor Carrow had said nothing to Vivian then.

He still said nothing when his daughter returned to him a changed and altered person whose laughter was forgotten and whose eyes brimmed with unshed tears.

"Is there anything you would like to do today?" the Professor asked. "I could play truant from my work if you like, and we could go off somewhere this afternoon."

Vivian shook her head.

"No, thank you, Daddy," she replied. "I think I will sit in the garden. I have got some sewing I want to do."

With a little sigh the Professor took up the letters which lay beside the morning paper. He had made his offer and it had been rejected.

He could not think of anything else to relieve the tension which lay between them.

The first letters he opened were bills and he passed them across to Vivian, who invariably saw to all his accounts.

The third letter, however, he read and re-read before speaking, and when he did so it was in a voice serious and slightly apprehensive.

"This is of the utmost importance, Vivian, my dear," he said. "And yet I hardly know what I am to say?"

"What is it?" Vivian asked, looking up from the accounts which she was reading carefully.

"It is a letter asking me to go to a very strange country," the Professor said.

"Where?" Vivian asked with some interest.

The Professor hesitated, reading the letter yet again before he answered.

"Tell me, Daddy," Vivian said impatiently. "Are we to go soon?"

"I do not know what to think," murmured the Professor. "And I certainly don't think it is a case of 'we.'"

"What do you mean?" Vivian asked sharply.

"I mean, my dear," the Professor said, "that if I accept this proposition—a very extraordinary one indeed—there would be no question of you accompanying me."

"In which case, then, you would not go," Vivian said easily.

"That is the whole point," Professor Carrow went on. "I do not think I can refuse. It has been put to me that this is a service I can do for England. In fact they are sending someone from the War Office down to see me tomorrow."

He looked again at the letter.

"No, by Jove! He is arriving today. A Captain Alexander. The letter says that he will explain everything."

"But don't they tell you where it is that they want you to go?" Vivian said, interested now almost in spite of herself.

"To Tibet," the Professor answered.

"To Tibet," Vivian echoed. "I thought no white people were allowed in, that the country was closed to foreigners of all sorts."

"So I believed," the Professor answered. "And that is why we must wait for the arrival of Captain Alexander."

Vivian rose to her feet.

"Will he be here to lunch?" she asked.

"I should think so, my dear," the Professor answered, "the letter says he will arrive about noon by aeroplane, weather permitting."

"He would come the one day we were having shepherd's pie," Vivian said. "I had better go and see Nanny and find out if we can change the menu."

At the doorway she paused and looked back at the Professor, seated with his glasses on his nose, staring anxiously at the letter in his hand.

"Daddy," she said, in a firm, clear voice, and then waited until he glanced at her.

31

"Yes, my dear?" he answered.

"I am going with you," she said, "whether you go to Tibet, Timbuctoo, or the bottom of the sea. Get that quite clearly into your mind from the very beginning."

A sudden smile dimpled her face and transformed her again into the Vivian of a fortnight ago.

She blew her father a kiss and went out, shutting the door behind her before he could reply.

For five or six minutes the Professor sat thinking deeply, staring with unseeing eyes across the yellow-walled dining room, then he rose to his feet and went pensively to his study.

He took down his atlas and gazed at the map of that mysterious, almost unknown country north of India, then he looked at a cutting which lay in a drawer beside his desk.

It announced in a sensational inaccurate fashion that the Dalai Lama of Tibet, the reincarnation of Buddha and the nominal ruler of three million inhabitants was dead.

All that morning, the Professor turned over books and maps seeking with little success for information about the most amazing country in the world, and in the end he had learned little more than he knew already.

It was with relief that just before twelve o'clock he heard the noise of an aeroplane overhead and watched it, five minutes later, land in a meadow a little way from the house.

He walked slowly across the garden towards the fields and was joined by Vivian.

They could see the pilot clambering out from the plane taking off his helmet. Then the Professor found his arm gripped tightly by his daughter while she said:

"Promise me one thing, Daddy."

"What is that?" her father said affectionately.

"That if you make up your mind to go, whether I can accompany you or not, you will ask that someone may go with you to transcribe your maps."

"Oh, I dare say I can manage it by myself," the Professor said. "Granted I have not done it for years, my dear — thanks to you; but I expect I can fall back into the old habits of drawing them out myself."

"Promise me you will ask," Vivian said. "I have a

reason for saying this. Promise me, Daddy. It isn't much to ask."

The Professor hesitated for a moment, then replied, "I promise," just as the airman came within earshot.

Broad shouldered, with dark hair brushed back from a square forehead, with deep-set eyes in an interesting face, Captain Alexander shook hands with the Professor and then with Vivian.

"I am so sorry to arrive with so little preliminary notice. I am afraid you only got the chief's letter this morning. I do hope I have not upset your plans."

"Luckily we lead a very quiet life here," the Professor answered, "so you were not likely to find us out."

"In which case I suppose I should have had to wait until you returned," Captain Alexander said cheerfully.

As they all three walked towards the house, Vivian glanced at him curiously. She felt somehow vaguely that she had met him before and yet could not place him.

He gave a surprising impression of strength. He was obviously an athletic man, and he had a brisk, quick manner.

He hardly spoke to Vivian, keeping his conversation for the Professor so that it was almost with a little attitude of reproach that Vivian said:

"I have ordered lunch for you, Captain Alexander. I hope that your talk with my father will not take more than an hour."

"I am sorry," Captain Alexander replied, "but that is quite impossible, Miss Carrow. I have got to get back to London immediately I have talked to the Professor."

"But that is absurd," the Professor expostulated. "Of course you must stay to lunch, my dear fellow. You have got to eat somewhere."

"I am afraid I shall not do so today," Captain Alexander said; "unless, of course, Miss Carrow likes to do me up a few sandwiches. That would be very kind of her.

Something in his smile as he referred to her in the third person annoyed Vivian.

She came to the conclusion that this young man was far too sure of himself, far too busy leading his own life without reference to the feelings of others.

It was not so much, she told herself, annoying that she

had wasted the morning preparing extra dishes for lunch, but his almost smug satisfaction in his own busyness.

What was more, she was irritated by that faint sense of familiarity which she could not place.

"Very well," she said quietly. "If you prefer it, you can have a few sandwiches."

Without waiting for his thanks she walked towards the kitchen.

Once there, however, she gave the order swiftly to Jean, then hurrying back through the hall on tip-toe she let herself out into the garden.

The library window was open and she could hear the sound of their voices. Nearer and nearer she crept until she was directly outside it.

Noiselessly she moved a garden cushion. Placing it in position she sat so that her shoulders were against the wall of the house and her ears on a level with the old-fashioned lead window with its diamond panes.

"We have not forgotten, sir," Captain Alexander was saying, "the splendid work you did for us in Africa, and after the revolution in China."

"That was a long time ago," the Professor interposed.

"I know," Captain Alexander said; "and yet you would hardly believe how very few alterations have had to be made to your maps. A town here or there has been deserted or moved because of the course of the river, but otherwise they are unchanged. There is no one to touch you in that particular branch of your work."

"I am sorry to hear that," the Professor said. "The young fellows must come on, you know. I am not as young as I was."

"There is no one, sir," Captain Alexander said. "And that is why I have got to ask you to do this great service for us. There is no one who could even attempt the task of making a map of Tibet, let alone add the knowledge of mineralogy, which in this instance is highly important."

"Perhaps you had better explain to me from the beginning," the Professor said gently, "so that I shall know exactly where we stand."

"Certainly it would be the best," the Captain answered.

As Vivian had listened she had stiffened and with difficulty prevented herself from giving an audible exclamation.

She had indeed half started to her feet in surprise before

34

she remembered her position and crouched down again in silence.

Hearing Captain Alexander without seeing him had revealed the origin of that strange familiarity which she had felt in his presence.

She had not recognized him because she had never seen him before; but now, listening, she knew exactly who he was.

The man who had come to her in the darkness of the night in that summerhouse at Monte Carlo.

CHAPTER FOUR

"We must go back," said Captain Alexander, "to the early years of this century, when Tibet was in suzerainty to China, and both Russia and Britain were toying with the idea of gaining an advantage in this country of completely undeveloped wealth."

He smiled and went on:

"You will remember, of course, that a Russian named Dorgieff bamboozled the Dalai Lama into believing that the Czar and the whole Russian Empire were about to embrace the Buddhist religion and come under the spiritual rule of Lhasa."

"A lie!" the Professor interposed.

"In consequence of these lies," Captain Alexander continued, "the Dalai Lama sent back unopened the letters addressed to him by the Viceroy of India.

"Becoming alarmed, the British sent an expedition to Lhasa which, having captured Gyangtse, journeyed on to the capital, only to find the Dalai Lama had fled to Mongolia."

He paused.

"However, treaties were finally drawn up by which Britain and Russia agreed not to mine in or seek to take any part in the ruling of Tibet.

"With the exception that we should be allowed certain

mart stations including one at Gyangtse, about one hundred and fifty miles in the interior of the country."

"I remember that," the Professor remarked.

"From the moment these treaties were signed, Tibet fell back into an uncivilized, isolated state from which she has never emerged," Captain Alexander said.

"The progression of the last thirty years has passed unnoticed in the country, which is closed to tourists and to all foreigners save a few Chinese.

"It is an amazing state of affairs to think that such a place does exist in the world today. To know that we can fly to Australia, can land in India, can telephone Los Angeles or Cape Town, but that one cannot even look at an authentic map of an enormous state in the centre of Asia is almost unbelievable.

"But there is a much more serious side to it than the fact that five million people are being brought up in ignorance of so-called civilization."

Captain Alexander paused, and Vivian could hear the Professor move in his chair.

"Cigarette?" her father asked. "Go on. You are interesting me very much."

"As you have seen in the newspapers, the Dalai Lama is dead," Captain Alexander continued after a moment. "The Lamas are seeking his reincarnation and they should find him within this year or the next.

"It is no easy task, the child has to be born with the marks of a tiger skin on his legs, two pieces of flesh near the shoulder-blades suggesting hands, and a shell-like imprint on one palm.

"It is also politically to the advantage of the various monasteries, who own the majority of the land, to find him within their own environments.

"You can imagine the trouble they take for the accomplishment of this and the amount of death and destruction which goes on amongst themselves.

"It is a well-known fact that very few of the Dalai Lamas ever live to attain their majority.

"Their Regents hate giving up the power of rulership, and it is not very extraordinary that Dalai Lama after Dalai Lama dies at the age of seventeen.

"Poisoning is an accomplished art in Tibet; there are

several poisons employed by Tibetans which are completely unknown in Europe.

"Before the Younghusband Expedition they always fought with poisoned arrows.

"Now they have a large standing army carrying rifles which have been copied from ours so skilfully and with such an eye for detail that even the original makers' names have been added."

The Professor laughed.

"But let us come to the point," Captain Alexander went on. "The last Dalai Lama did nothing to improve the country or utilize the enormous mineral resources which lie completely undeveloped, stupendous but useless wealth.

"When one considers the miserable and pitiful plight of the peasants who can barely scrape a living from the land, the whole thing sounds like a fairy-tale.

"The Dalai Lama, by jealously guarding the spiritual rule of the country, and closing the frontiers to the material world outside, knew that he personally could remain supreme.

"But since his death two years ago, various of the huge monasteries whose monks, although they call themselves Buddhists, are not at all averse to taking life have begun to grumble that such natural wealth as the country possesses is not being used for their advantage."

"It is not surprising," the Professor murmured.

"Russia has always wanted to flirt with Tibet," Captain Alexander continued. "No one knows better than she the wealth of the mines, and also how easy it would be to open the Tibetan frontiers to Soviet Russia.

"We have been informed that secret negotiations are going forward between a Russian syndicate and one of the largest monasteries in Tibet.

"We do not know anything definite, of course, for a spy system is amazingly difficult and exceedingly complicated to maintain and our hands are tied by the fact that we have practically no maps of the country.

"For the Younghusband Expedition, maps had been made by the '*pandits*' who took their lives in their hands so that they might enter the country disguised as holy men or merchants and take what bearings they could.

"You know their story. Twirling their prayer-wheels,

which were covered not with prayers but with compass bearings, they moved about the country, using rosaries for pacing out the distances."

The Professor smiled.

"It was amazing what they accomplished with such primitive methods," Captain Alexander remarked. "But I need not point out to you, sir how, inaccurate such information is bound to be. And, of course, no one knows exactly where the gold mines are.

"We are told there is enough gold to swamp the world and ruin its value for ever. Whether that is true or not we cannot say.

"One thing is quite certain—Britain cannot allow any infringement of the peace terms which she herself has drawn up for Tibet.

"It is for this reason, Professor, that we have appealed to you to help us."

"But if no one is allowed in?" the Professor asked.

"That is, of course, an enormous difficulty," Captain Alexander answered. "But, as I have said before, there is a British mart station at Gyangtse, a hundred and fifty miles in the interior.

"As it happens, it is not so very far from the monastery which constitutes the main danger at the moment. It is, therefore, within that particular province that we think any mining is likely to take place.

"Now our idea is this. We get you a pass to visit Gyangtse as the guest of Mr. Andrews, the British trade agent. This is not, as a matter of fact, difficult.

"You will travel by the known trade route over the frontier to the town in question. When you are there it is up to you to do what you can for us in the surrounding country.

"It will not be easy. I am not pretending that it will be; but we have certain people who will do their best to assist you in every way."

"When would you want me to leave?" the Professor asked.

"At once," Captain Alexander answered. "September is the best time to cross the Sikkim Pass, and also, if I may say so, there is no time to be lost. Prevention is better than cure, as you know, in all exploits like this.

"A firm hand taken at the very beginning of an intrigue will often quench it altogether.

"We do not know what is afoot, but our motto is to be prepared for anything. Please don't fail us, sir.

"You are our greatest hope. There is no one else who can do the work that you can do, and there is no one else that we can turn to at this moment."

There was a long pause. Vivian, listening at the window, could almost feel the tension between the two men.

She could visualize Captain Alexander bending forward eagerly in an attitude of supplication; her father sitting, as he always did when concentrating, with the two first fingers of both hands pressed against his temples.

"You cannot give me any time to think it over?" the Professor asked at length, breaking a silence of several minutes.

"I am afraid not, sir," Captain Alexander replied. "It will take some time to get the pass and, as you may imagine, we do not want to show any undue anxiety to hustle things through.

"The more casual the whole trip seems, the better it will be. I know, of course, there will be various things you will want to get which will take time.

"I should suggest that your clothes and big baggage should go by sea on the *Corinthia,* sailing on Monday for Calcutta.

"It would be better and would save comment if you yourself would fly. The last thing we want is any newspaper publicity about your leaving England for India.

"It is not likely that any construction would be put on such a statement, but one never knows.

"You will have to pass through the semi-independent State of Sikkim to get to the frontier. They, of course, have their spies, who report anything unusual to Lhasa immediately."

With a sigh the Professor rose to his feet.

"Very well, Captain Alexander," he said. "I accept. I shall leave all the arrangements in your hands."

"I cannot thank you enough, sir," the young man said eagerly. "I will get back to London immediately with my good news."

"Oh, and by the way," the Professor added, as if he had suddenly remembered something. "I shall want to take an assistant with me. I am afraid my eyes are not what they used to be and the tracing and preparing of maps is, I find, too heavy a task these days and too intricate a one for me personally."

"But I am afraid—" Captain Alexander started.

"Without an assistant," the Professor interrupted, "I fear I shall be little use to you."

Captain Alexander sighed, and Vivian listening eagerly outside, could almost hear him shrug his shoulders.

"Very good, sir, if you insist," came the reply. "But you will choose someone absolutely reliable? There is no need for me to tell you that everything I have said is completely in confidence.

"One word noised abroad of all this might be the death of all our hopes of the future, besides doing incalculable harm."

"Oh, of course," the Professor answered. "That goes without saying."

There was a moment's pause and he went on:

"I will just get you a drink before you go and see if your sandwiches are ready."

Vivian heard the library door open and close. Very stealthily she started to creep away from her listening post. But she had hardly moved a few feet before a voice at the window made her jump.

"Do you always listen to your father's interviews, Miss Carrow?"

She turned to face Captain Alexander seated on the lead window seat.

For a moment she had no answer ready, and then, raising her chin high, she faced him defiantly:

"It saves him a lot of trouble in telling me the whole story afterwards," she said coldly.

"Then it would have been more honest for you to have suggested coming in at the very beginning," Captain Alexander retorted. "As a matter of fact I nearly invited you. I heard you move at the start of our conversation. I don't think you would make a good spy, Miss Carrow."

Vivian flushed with anger.

41

"I hope it is a thing I shall never have to sink to," she answered. "Even you must find it very exhausting."

Captain Alexander raised his eyebrows and looked at her with what seemed almost amusement in his dark eyes.

"I am sorry you did not get my flowers," he said quietly.

Vivian, who had been turning over in her mind whether she should let him know that she had recognized him, almost started.

She had received the card from her aunt with the two simple words on it two days after her arrival home.

But she had been too overcome by her grief to give it more than a passing thought, and she had thrown it into the wastepaper basket.

"So they were from you," she said aloud. "I thought they might be."

"Of course they were," he answered with a smile. "I am a very grateful person when people do what I want them to do."

"And do they often do that?" Vivian asked.

"Always," he answered.

She was stung by the confidence in his voice. She told herself that he was insufferably conceited.

"I do hope that one day you will be disappointed," she said with a rather bitter smile. "I think everyone finds that their best plans go astray sooner or later."

"I am sorry you have no good wishes for me, for I am feeling rather pleased with myself at the moment," he answered.

"Because you have got my father to agree to what you want?" Vivian asked. "That was not your doing—it was because he feels he might be of service to his country."

"But of course," Captain Alexander said.

There was the sound of the library door opening and he sprang to his feet.

"Oh, thank you very much, sir," Vivian heard him say as he disappeared inside the room. "It is kind of you. You should not have troubled."

Slowly she retraced her steps to the front of the house and stood for a moment looking towards the field where Captain Alexander's aeroplane awaited him, and then she turned and walked indoors and upstairs to her bedroom.

"That man is insufferable," she told her looking glass, as she tidied her hair with deft fingers.

A few moments later she heard the aeroplane take off. She ran quickly downstairs to her father, smiling almost happily for the first time since she had returned home from Monte Carlo.

She hurried into the library where he was sitting in his favorite armchair, smoking a pipe, deep in concentration and looking worried.

She slipped her arm round his neck and kissed the bald patch on the top of his head.

"Now, darling," she said gaily, "we begin to make plans."

"Don't be ridiculous, Vivian," the Professor answered. "It is quite impossible for you to accompany me."

"My sweet," his daughter replied, "I am going to take your heavy luggage by sea on Monday. You will journey by air and we shall meet at Darjeeling. Ostensibly, I shall be going to stay with that exceedingly dull cousin of yours, Colonel Humphreys. It is all so simple. I have got it all cut and dried."

"It is quite impossible," the Professor said sternly.

Vivian moved away from his chair and stood with her back to him looking out across the garden.

"Daddy," she said very quietly, after a moment, "do you know why I came back from Monte Carlo?"

"No," he answered. "I thought you would very likely tell me in your own good time."

"I came back," Vivian said steadily, "because Jimmy Loring is going to marry the Stubbs girl."

Her voice broke on the last word but she turned swiftly round to face her father.

"Don't you see, Daddy, don't you understand? I cannot be in England when they return. I cannot be here when they are married. Hear about it . . . read about it in the papers . . . see pictures . . ."

With tears in her eyes and tears choking her voice, for a moment Vivian hesitated, and then she moved and fell on her knees beside her father.

His arms went out to hold her and her face was hidden against his shoulder.

"Darling, darling," she choked, "you do understand, don't you?"

The Professor did not answer, but his arms held her very closely.

Vivian knew whatever difficulties stood in the way, whatever barriers had to be surmounted, she had her father's permission to travel with him to Tibet.

CHAPTER FIVE

People of all sorts and descriptions were hurrying up the sharply inclined gangway leading into the bowels of the ship, where they were received by the white-coated stewards.

Officers, resplendent in gold lace, were keeping a sharp lookout for the more important passengers who had to be welcomed aboard.

"You are right, you know," Vivian remarked.

"About what?" the Professor inquired.

"People's fear of motion," Vivian answered. "You remember how we discussed it last time we went abroad? I have never forgotten the conversation and your theory that traveling is an innovation of this century, and that few people seem to have become acclimatized as yet."

The Professor laughed—a low, quick sound which was characteristic of him.

It was time for those who were not traveling to leave the ship and Vivian felt a sudden sinking of her spirits.

She had three weeks on board ahead of her with, so far as she knew, not one single person of her acquaintance as a companion.

"I wish you were coming, darling," she said to her father. "It will seem ages until we meet again and start our adventure."

"Don't say it too loud," the Professor answered. "I cannot tell you how guilty I feel about all this plotting and planning."

"Now don't start worrying," Vivian replied affectionately. "It is all going to be all right."

"If I think there is any real danger, I reserve the right to forbid you to go, even at the last moment," the Professor said.

"In which case I shan't allow you to go either," Vivian replied firmly.

The Professor sighed in mock heroism.

"I fear that you are a very badly brought up child," he said. "I cannot think why I wasn't stricter with you."

Vivian laughed, put her arms round him, and kissed him.

"I may as well start kissing you now," she said, "there is the bugle."

They moved slowly down the deck towards the companionway leading to the lounge.

In the doorway, they stood aside to allow one of the chief officers to pass through, a retinue of turbaned Indians in his wake.

"I wonder who these are?" Vivian asked.

As she spoke one of the group, a young man of about twenty-four, wearing European dress, stepped forward and spoke to the Professor.

"Professor Carrow!" he exclaimed. "How are you? I did not know we were to have the pleasure of your company on this ship."

"You are not," the Professor said, shaking him by the hand; "but I am very pleased to see you again. And how is your father?"

"He is very well, I am glad to say," the young man answered, "getting ready for his Jubilee next year. They are already polishing the State jewels and brushing up the elephants."

"I don't think you know my daughter," the Professor said. "Vivian, this is Prince Kowa. You remember that some years ago I stayed with his father, the Khan of Bhulusta."

The Prince turned eagerly to Vivian.

"The Professor was invaluable," he said. "Due entirely to his work and the finding of several sapphire mines, the Bhulusta fortunes are doing well."

"You are very kind," the Professor murmured. "But

tell me about yourself, dear boy. What are you doing in England?"

"It took me until this year," the Prince said, "to persuade my father to allow me to come over here on a visit, and never have I enjoyed anything so much."

"You persevered with your English," the Professor said.

"Oh, you remember my old Scotch tutor," the Prince answered with a laugh. "He is still at home. He is teaching my younger brother now. But you are not coming on this ship?"

"I am afraid not," the Professor answered. "My daughter only is traveling this time. She is going to Calcutta."

"Then I hope I may avail myself of the privilege of seeing her later," the Prince said with a bow.

He flashed his dark eyes at Vivian and with another hearty handshake with the Professor, he moved on to where his suite were awaiting him.

"He speaks English amazingly well," Vivian said as they moved down towards the lower deck.

"His father is a most bigoted old man," the Professor replied. "His State on the border of Afghanistan is backward entirely due to his prejudice against European civilization of any sort. But his children refused to be repressed. The eldest son, who is married, spends several months of the year in Paris. This one, Kowa, I believe is a very wild boy who was always in disgrace.

"However, I am not surprised that he got his own way. The Khan is getting old and cares of State take up too much of his time these days for him to be able to cope with domestic upheavals as well."

"Is he a good ruler?" Vivian asked.

"Not particularly," the Professor replied. "But I remember feeling in Bhulusta as if I was completely isolated from the world—past, present and future. I told you about it at the time."

"I remember your going there well," Vivian said. "And how furious I was that I couldn't accompany you."

"All ashore," called the stewards, moving the mass of people slowly and relentlessly down the gangway.

Women were crying openly, men were already waving farewell with that forced cheerfulness with which Englishmen hide their deepest feelings.

Children were shouting shrill, unintelligible messages to

47

their parents and relations leaning over the side. The sailors were getting ready to take away the gangways.

"Good-bye, my darling," the Professor said to Vivian, holding her closely to him for a last embrace. "Take care of yourself, and God bless you."

Vivian clung to him for a moment and then watched him walk slowly ashore. She felt suddenly forlorn and near to tears.

"Good-bye," she called. Her words were lost amid the clanging crash of the gangways being lowered to the quay.

Slowly, very slowly, the ship began to head for the open sea. Vivian waved for a little while and then, long before anyone else, she turned and made her way to her cabin.

It was one of her few superstitions never to see a train, a ship, or someone she loved, taken out of sight.

The Professor, who knew this fancy of hers, was already preparing to move out of the crowd and find a taxi which would take him back to the station and so to London.

They had planned together, father and daughter, the whole of their movements for the next few weeks until they should find themselves safely over the frontier and into Tibet.

Once the Professor had agreed to Vivian accompanying him he not only made no further difficulties but joined her plotting with meticulous care so that no false step should defeat their aims.

Vivian was to land at Calcutta and to go from there straight up to Darjeeling.

There the Professor would join her by aeroplane, armed with the passes which would carry them through Sikkim. At Darjeeling they would receive further permits from the Tibetan authorities to visit Gyangtse.

Captain Alexander had lost no time on arrival in London, and his chief had telephoned the Professor that same evening to make arrangements and ask the Professor to visit him as soon as possible.

The Professor had told him then that it was exceedingly fortunate that his daughter had already planned a trip to India and it made no difference to her to sail on Monday with his big luggage, which she could deposit for him to pick up when he arrived by air.

"He thinks it is a splendid idea," the Professor said to Vivian when he related the conversation. "He is very anxious that I should have as little as possible to pass through the customs either here or in Calcutta.

"The less notice that is taken of me the better, while you can travel with compasses, sextants, and cameras without anyone being unduly suspicious."

"In fact, darling," Vivian replied gaily, "they are only too delighted to make use of me, in which case they mustn't be surprised if we turn the tables on them."

"I expect I shall get into awful trouble over this," the Professor said; "but still it is worth it, if only to see you smile again."

Vivian flushed, and then with an effort she forced herself to meet her father's eyes.

"From the moment I leave England," she promised him, "what is past shall be dead and forgotten."

But it was easier for her to say that than for her to keep her promise as she saw the coast of England becoming smaller and smaller in the distance.

After dinner she put on a thick coat and walked out on deck. From behind her, in the brilliantly lighted lounge, came the sound of music, the laughter and voices of dancers.

While from the open portholes of the bar she could hear the clatter of glasses and the clinking of ice in the cocktail shakers.

Vivian was very small and lonely beside the vast expanse of sea and sky. She felt a sudden overwhelming desire for Jimmy.

Fiercely Vivian derided herself for the emotions which swept over her at the mere thought of him.

Scornfully she told herself to remember that he had jilted her, thrown her aside, not for love but for mere mercenary advantage.

"Dear God, help me to forget," Vivian prayed.

She raised her face to the dark sky above her, closed her eyes and listened beneath all the noise to the soothing sound of the waves against the ship's sides.

Then a voice at her side spoke gently, a voice charming and cultured, yet the slurring of the words, ever so slightly, gave it a strange, attractive, un-English accent.

"May I speak with you, Miss Carrow?" the voice said. "Or am I interrupting a very pleasant reverie?"

49

Vivian started; then turned to find Prince Kowa at her side.

* * * *

"When you look sad, you are very beautiful," Prince Kowa said solemnly; "and when you smile you are very beautiful also. I don't know to which I would give the prize."

Vivian laughed. She was lying in a deck chair, a striped rug tucked round her, and the Prince was sitting next to her, similarly wrapped.

The breeze was cold but the sun was glorious as they steamed in the Mediterranean.

"I think you are ridiculous!" Vivian said.

But she smiled as she spoke and there was no annoyance in her tone at his flattery.

"Why do English women," asked the Prince, "always protest when one tells them nice things? If one is unkind or critical they say—'I am afraid you are right,' or 'Yes, it is kind of you to tell me,' but if one tells them a pleasing truth they object. In my country it is different."

"I think flattery is always embarrassing," Vivian said. "I suppose we are not used to it. Our men are not very complimentary as a rule."

"Oh, I don't understand your men," the Prince said. "Your father, yes, and my tutor. They are splendid, and I believe that what they do and what they think are right; but they are old men. I speak of men of my own age.

"In Bhulusta we live, we love, we get married and still we love, but in England your men, what do they do? Play golf—always. Everything and every woman is sacrificed to the golf course. It is a strange God and undoubtedly a very jealous one."

"How long have you been in England?" Vivian asked.

"Four months," the Prince replied.

"And yet you are judging us so severely on such a short acquaintance? I think you are very hasty."

"If I ask you your opinion on my country I am quite certain you would give it to me," he parried.

"I expect I should," Vivian retorted.

"And that would be all right," he said pensively, "because you are English, and an English person's judgment is correct whatever his knowledge of the facts. But a mere foreigner, he must not express an opinion because that is presumptuous."

"Again I think you are being ridiculous," Vivian said lazily; "but I am too sleepy to argue."

She did not take the Prince very seriously.

Already she had heard many of his ideas; some she laughed at, some she realized were the hastily-formed judgments of an impetuous youth, and many were due to the age-old antagonism created by racial prejudice.

But the Prince amused her and undoubtedly the days passed more quickly in his company.

He had not attempted to disguise the fact that he found Vivian exceedingly attractive and was prepared to seek her company on every possible occasion.

Prince Kowa, with his eager chatter, helped Vivian to pass many long hours when she would have been unable to escape from her own thoughts, and she was grateful to him in an amused, tolerant, way.

The Anglo-Indians, the Colonels' wives, and the tea-planters who made up the majority of the passengers on the ship, voiced their disapproval of her behavior in no uncertain terms.

Vivian would have had to be blind not to notice the disapproval on their plain, respectable faces as she walked the deck escorted by the Prince, or took part in the deck games with him as a partner.

"Do you realize you are making me lose my reputation?" she said to him jokingly.

She was surprised at the storm her words aroused, for clenching his fists and frowning until his dark eyebrows met across the thin bridge of his nose, he said vehemently:

"Curse them! Curse the whole damn lot of them. What right have they even to speak of you? I wish they were of my own people and I could have them tortured for their impudence."

"Don't be such a barbarian," Vivian said. "It doesn't matter, does it?"

"You are so good, so much above them all," the Prince answered. "I cannot bear to mention you with the same breath as I speak of them. Those pale-faced, withered creatures, burnt and shriveled by the hot sun until there is nothing left in them but the venom of their tongues."

"But this is marvelous. What a sentence!" Vivian said,

51

clapping her hands. "Will you promise me to repeat it to your tutor? He would be proud of his pupil."

"You are laughing at me," the Prince said.

Vivian had to hasten to reassure him she was not teasing to stop him sulking.

"What did you think of Dhilangi's suicide at Monte Carlo?" she asked to distract his thoughts.

"I think it was very convenient for the British Government," the Prince replied. "In fact, too convenient to be natural."

"You think he was murdered?" Vivian asked.

A cold feeling almost of fear was creeping over her.

"It would not be policy for me to say so," he answered, "but if you ask me, I think he was bumped off."

"Surely that is impossible outside America?" Vivian protested. "And if they had suspected murder, wouldn't the police have said so?"

"In London," the Prince said, "everyone was quite certain that Dhilangi had not died by his own hand. But they also said that at Monte Carlo the police will never allow a crime to take place if they can help it—it means bad business for the Casino."

Vivian was silent, and then she said:

"What was he like, Dhilangi? Did you know him?"

"I did meet him once," the Prince answered. "He was a strange person with an amazing power of rousing a crowd to fury and rebellion."

"Do you think it is a good thing he is dead?"

The Prince shrugged his shoulders.

"Who can say?" he replied. "Some of the things he demanded were undoubtedly just; others were, perhaps, too revolutionary."

For a long time that night Vivian could not sleep.

Over and over she turned in her mind the incident of Captain Alexander's appearance in the summerhouse of the Villa Belle Mere.

His instructions which she had so faithfully carried out, the gendarmes who had gone away thinking they had interrupted a lovers' quarrel, and the smear of blood she had discovered subsequently on her evening dress.

Had she done right or had she been wrong in acquiescing in the command of a stranger, English though he was?

Should she have told her father to have nothing to do with any proposition that Captain Alexander might bring, whether he was backed by the power and authority of the government or not?

Vivian had not mentioned the fact that she had met Captain Alexander before or that their acquaintanceship was any other than the few words they had spoken in the Professor's presence on his arrival at the Manor House.

Yet she shuddered and lay sleepless as she thought about him, and the more she thought the more she hated that strange, self-confident man, Captain Alexander.

The next day the sea was rough though the sun was shining brightly. One or two of the more hardy travellers among the women ventured out on deck.

Vivian was leaning over the rail watching the distant shore when a small woman of uncertain age, rather untidily dressed, spoke to her.

"You are the daughter of Professor Carrow, are you not?" she started the conversation. "My name is Mrs. Hunter. Let me introduce myself. My husband met your father some years ago in South Africa."

"Oh, did he?" Vivian said politely.

"In the meantime," Mrs. Hunter went on, "I hope you will forgive a word of advice from an older and more experienced woman. I think you have no mother, and as you are alone on this voyage, I know you will not think it presumptuous of me if I venture to speak to you as if I were a relation."

Vivian instantly thought it very presumptuous, but while she hesitated for words Mrs. Hunter went on:

"You see, my dear," she said, "knowing the East as I do —after thirty years one can't help but know the country— it is always pitiable to see strangers, especially young girls like yourself, starting off in the wrong way.

"You see, our social standards are very high, and quite rightly so, because one cannot be too careful, especially where the mixture of races is concerned.

"Although, of course, I am not suggesting there is anything in it, I do think that you are making yourself needlessly conspicuous, and it is my duty as an Englishwoman, and as my husband is an old friend of your father's, to give you a word of warning."

She would have spoken for some time more if Vivian had not interrupted her. Drawing herself up, she said clearly and distinctly:

"Thank you very much, but I prefer to choose my own friends and never to seek or accept the advice of strangers. You will excuse me."

With that she walked away leaving a discomfited and infuriated Mrs. Hunter staring after her.

* * * *

"Will you come ashore with me?" the Prince asked Vivian.

They were steaming into Alexandria, the harbor filled with craft of all nationalities and guarded by a great grey battleship flying the white ensign.

"I'd love to," Vivian answered. "I have always wanted to see Alexandria. It holds an amazingly romantic place in my mind."

"Because of Alexander the Great?" the Prince asked. "Is he such a hero to you with his big library and his research laboratories?"

"Oh, not because of him," Vivian said, "but because of Cleopatra. It was here she met Antony, and here she spent so much of her romantic and exciting life, and here she is supposed to be buried, although they have never found the right spot."

"I am not particularly an admirer of Cleopatra," the Prince said.

"That is not surprising," Vivian answered. "It is always amusing that where history is concerned men make heroes of their own sex while women love to admire the exploits of women. I remember so well being taught about Cleopatra, and making up my mind she was the one person I would wish to be like."

"Hardly a proper ideal for a respectable English Miss," the Prince said teasingly.

The conversation was cut short by the arrival of the ship at the quayside.

Vivian could keep her attention on nothing save the hordes of shouting, gesticulating natives screaming unintelligible remarks, running up the gangplanks, striving to attract the attention of the passengers with glittering necklaces of colored stones, carved ivory flywhisks, fruit and bunches of bright-colored flowers.

54

"I love the East," she said to the Prince. "I like the familiar smell of sand, of fruit and sandalwood, of black bodies and that peculiar fragrance which seems to come straight from the desert to the sea, however many cities it encounters in between."

As soon as the passengers were allowed ashore, Vivian and Prince Kowa clambered into one of the open Victorias which were waiting on the cobbled quayside.

They had the greatest difficulty in reaching one, for the moment they set foot on dry land they were beset by beggars, hawkers, and touts.

The Prince's native language was of no use here, but Vivian knew a few words of Arabic and when she spoke their route was cleared almost magically.

"They think they are dealing with an old and hardened *habitué,*" Vivian explained laughingly as they clambered into the Victoria, "and they are not half such good prey as an American arriving for the first time, or a timid little tourist who is terrified by their noise and persistence."

They ambled through the streets of the town, well laid out with modern buildings, so that, as Vivian said sadly, there was little to remind them of the glory that was past.

It was very hot, and they had ices in a small cafe, where the proprietor greeted them with so much delight and palaver that Vivian ate more than she wanted just to please him.

Leisurely they left the hot streets behind them and drove out to a little sandy bay where all Egyptian society congregates when the hot weather arrives.

Everyone was sunbathing or having their bodies oiled in the shade of the little striped bathing-tents.

"It looks almost like Monte Carlo, doesn't it?" the Prince said.

He did not understand why, with a sudden change in her voice, Vivian suggested that they should return to the ship.

The words "Monte Carlo" still had the power to make her feel a sudden sense of desolation and misery, to throw her out of tune with the beauty and sunshine around her.

"You are not angry with me?" the Prince said, suddenly interrupting her thoughts.

"Of course not," Vivian said. "Why should I be?"

"You were so silent and cold," he replied. "I just wondered."

There was something almost pathetic in the dark eyes which swept her face.

"I hope I shall never be angry with you," Vivian said.

He smiled, showing a perfect row of white teeth.

"He is really handsome," Vivian said to herself. "And somehow very un-Eastern."

Indeed, in the grey flannel suit with a white stripe which had been made in Savile Row, and a hat tipped forward over his eyes, except for the darkness of his skin Prince Kowa might have been any good-looking sunburned young Englishman at his University or with his Regiment.

His manners were perfect, his English, spoken with only the slightest accent on some of the more difficult words, was more extensive than that of many an Englishman of his own age.

He was well educated from the particular English point of view, his tutor having brought him up with a knowledge of all those things which are discussed and which are not discussed in general conversation. He was agreeable, he was intelligent.

More and more Vivian felt infuriated by the prejudice of such people as she had already encountered on the boat.

Such reflections made her unduly gracious as they stepped aboard once more.

Before she turned in the direction of her cabin Vivian put out her hand and said:

"I cannot tell you how grateful I am to you. I should not have enjoyed Alexandria so much if you had not been with me."

She was about to say something else when a man, standing a few steps from them at the open door which led on to the deck attracted her attention.

She looked up and the words died on her lips as she found herself looking into the deep-set eyes of Captain Alexander.

"Oh!" the exclamation seemed to ring out she was so surprised.

"How are you, Miss Carrow?" he asked entirely at his ease.

"I did not know you were to travel on the ship," Vivian stammered.

She did not know why it upset her so much except she had thought herself free of him.

"I am here—if you need me."

Vivian walked away.

"How ridiculous he is," she told herself. "He is the last person I would ever need!"

CHAPTER SIX

The passage through the Red Sea was almost unbearably hot. At night many of the passengers slept on deck under the star-strewn sky.

The ship moving through the still water hardly disturbed their dreams and it seemed to Vivian that often she was the only person awake on the whole of this vast modern mammoth of the ocean.

Beyond the few remarks at their first meeting she and Captain Alexander had barely exchanged a dozen words since he had come aboard.

As a matter of fact she saw very little of him. He rose before she did and apparently he took his meals at different times.

The sports deck and the cardroom were not honored by his presence, neither was the cocktail-bar, where most people congregated when the sun had gone down and where the most social time of the day was the half hour before dinner.

Yet somehow, quite inexplicable to herself, she felt continually conscious of his presence on board.

When she was talking to the Prince she would find herself glancing up as if at every moment she expected him to appear.

A murderer and a spy! Not a particularly pretty description of any man.

That he was a murderer Vivian was fully convinced, and that he was a member of the British Secret Service had been revealed to her by her father.

His presence on board made her unaccountably nervous as regards her own plans.

Why this should be so was as unreasonable as it was annoying, since the Professor had made it quite clear that Vivian was going to India on a visit, and there was no reason whatever for Captain Alexander to think otherwise.

The Professor had further added that the assistant who was accompanying him was already in India and would join him at Darjeeling.

Supposing Captain Alexander came to see them off? Vivian thought. Supposing he insisted on accompanying her father on the first stages of the journey?

Lying on her mattress now, her hands behind her head, she wondered if it was worth wasting her time and thoughts upon any man.

Bitterly she thought of Jimmy and the life he had chosen of luxury purchased by marriage into the Stubbs family.

Did idealism count for nothing? Was materialism greater than all faith and love when it came to self-sacrifice?

Vivian suddenly felt terribly lonely, small, unprotected, and insecure.

The world was too big, too troublesome, and too turbulent for her ever to understand or combat.

In self-pity rather than from deep emotion tears slowly began to fill her eyes and course down her cheeks.

A sudden footstep made her start, and almost angrily she turned to face this intruder on her thoughts—and then as swiftly turned her head away.

Once again Captain Alexander had come to her in the darkness. He was still wearing evening clothes, obviously not having been to bed.

"Am I disturbing you?" he said.

She shook her head and then, after a moment's pause, found her voice.

"No," she said clearly. "I was just going down below."

"Too hot for you to sleep?" he asked; and without waiting for her answer went on: "Do you mind if I smoke?"

"No, please do," she replied. "Yes, it is hot, even up here."

"It is very much worse below," Captain Alexander said with a kind of gruff grimness.

"Then why stay down there?" Vivian said lightly.

She had complete control of her tears and herself by this time.

"Some poor devils cannot help it," Captain Alexander replied.

"What do you mean?" Vivian asked with curiosity. "Is somebody ill—is that why?"

She stopped, afraid of seeming too curious or importunate.

"Yes, that is why I have not been to bed," Captain Alexander said. "My servant is very ill."

"I am sorry," Vivian said simply. "Is there anything I can do?"

"Nothing. And it is nothing infectious, so don't be worried," he answered.

"I never thought of it," Vivian said scornfully. "I am not afraid of things like that."

There was a long pause between them, and only the glow of Captain Alexander's cigarette flickered like some live creature in the dimness.

It was he who broke the silence at last, and when he spoke his voice was low and curiously sympathetic.

"So you are still unhappy?" he said.

Vivian stiffened antagonistically for a moment and then her answer came as gently as his question.

"Yes, very," she said naturally.

"What is this thing called love?" Captain Alexander quoted almost beneath his breath.

"How do you know that it is love making me unhappy?" Vivian asked, a hint of anger in her voice.

"I have just watched a man dying because of it," he replied.

"Your servant?" Vivian asked. "But I thought he was ill."

Captain Alexander suddenly stirred and threw his cigarette into the sea, the point of light floating down and down like a tiny meteor to the water below.

Abruptly, and in a different voice altogether he said:

"I am going to turn in now. I am tired. Good night, Miss Carrow."

"Good night," Vivian echoed, slightly surprised at his swift change of attitude.

Then almost before the words were out of his mouth he disappeared down the companionway and she was alone.

She did not see him again the next day or the next.

"I hear Captain Alexander's servant is ill," she said to the stewardess on the third morning. "How is he?"

The stewardess gave her a strangely startled glance—at least, so it seemed to Vivian.

"I'm afraid I have not heard, Miss," she said primly.

She whisked out of the room before Vivian could question her further.

It seemed to Vivian that the ship had suddenly become unbearably dull.

"I wish there was something new to do" she said to the Prince. "I am getting tired of everyone's face. The fat woman who ogles the captain, the thin girl who looks like starving Russia, the timid colonial with his disagreeable wife."

"But you have forgotten the stout gentleman who is travelling in woolens," he said. "And the American mother and daughter who have made up their minds to disapprove of everything but to miss nothing."

"Talking of disapproval," Vivian went on, "thank heaven there are only another few days in which I have to bear Mrs. Hunter's baleful glances."

"Forget them," the Prince said. "Why not come down and sit in my sitting-room after dinner. I have got some interesting things to show you."

"What sort of things?" Vivian asked lazily.

She was not particularly interested and she wanted time to consider the invitation.

"There are some really good American records, for one thing," the Prince answered.

Vivian laughed.

"I thought at least you were going to offer me blood-red rubies or yards of pearls the size of marbles," she said.

"I wish I could show you my father's treasury," the Prince answered. "But I could show you some photographs of the palace if that would interest you."

"I would love to see them," Vivian replied. "Why not bring them up here in the cool?"

61

"No, come down to my suite," the Prince answered. "What does it matter? Surely you are not afraid?"

"Afraid?" Vivian echoed. "What of? The spiteful tongues of Mrs. Hunter and her kind. Of course I am not."

"Then I have thought of a really good idea," the Prince said enthusiastically. "Come and dine tomorrow night. I will order a special dinner just for you and me."

"Oh, I don't know," Vivian said doubtfully.

"Say yes!" he pleaded. "I am sure you are sick to death of the food in the dining-room. Why not join me just for once? After all, what does it matter what people say?"

"I have told you I don't care," Vivian said angrily.

"Then why are you hesitating?" the Prince persisted.

"All right," Vivian said, "I will come."

The following day, her afternoon *siesta* finished, she came up on deck to find the place almost deserted save for Captain Alexander reading the *Illustrated London News,* a battered panama hat pulled low over his eyebrows.

As she had to pass within a few feet of him, courtesy made Vivian stop and say:

"I hope your servant is better."

He sprang to his feet.

"Oh, Miss Carrow," he said quickly. "I am glad to see you. In fact you are the one person I wanted to see. That is why I was waiting here."

"Really!" Vivian said in an amused voice.

"Won't you sit down?" Captain Alexander suggested.

He pulled up a chair near his own and Vivian sank gracefully down upon it.

In her thin white tussore dress she looked cool and very attractive, but the sleepless nights and her unhappiness had left their mark in the shape of dark purple lines under her eyes.

"Miss Carrow," Captain Alexander began almost as soon as they were seated, "I do not want you to think I am presumptuous or in any way impertinent, but I would suggest to you that it would be much wiser if you did not dine with the Prince in his suite tonight."

"And may I ask why not?" Vivian said, her languor gone now.

"Certainly you may ask why," Captain Alexander said.

"And it is a question I can answer. Because you know that it is not a wise or advisable thing to do."

"Really," Vivian said, by now very angry, "I am afraid I must ask you not to interfere in things that do not concern you."

She made a movement to get up from her deckchair.

"Wait a moment," Captain Alexander said, putting out a hand and touching her arm. "Let me beg of you to be sensible over this. I have lived in the East all my life and I assure you that I am not talking rubbish when I tell you that it is not wise for any attractive girl to spend too much of her time in the company of a young man like Prince Kowa."

"The Prince is my friend," Vivian said hotly. "I like him, and I have found him superior in a great many ways to many of the white men I have met."

"That's as may be," was the reply. "The point is I must beg of you, Miss Carrow, as your father is not here and I cannot appeal to him, to put off this dinner-party this evening."

"If my father were here," Vivian said, "I should ask him, Captain Alexander, to tell you to mind your own business. Whether I dine with the Prince or not cannot have anything to do with you, and why you should trouble yourself over me I do not know."

She rose to her feet and faced him defiantly. She was very nearly as tall as he, but she felt that he was a formidable foe, and it made her all the more determined to vanquish him now and forever.

"I hope that is quite clear," Vivian said.

Captain Alexander did not answer.

"Of course," she continued softly. "I might inquire how you found out that I was intending to dine with the Prince, but perhaps that would be inquiring too closely into your business of espionage."

As she finished speaking her heart gave a sudden leap as she realized that Captain Alexander was really angry at her last words.

She saw a steely glint come into his deep-set eyes, a sudden tightening of his mouth.

He made a quick movement and just for one absurd, fanciful moment Vivian felt afraid he might be going to shake her.

Then almost before she had time to realize how ridiculous was such a fear she heard him say:

"You little fool!"

Turning, he walked abruptly away from her. Vivian watched him go and then almost shaking with anger she went into the writing room.

"How dare he speak to me like that?" she asked herself.

If only her father were here! If only in some way she could find words or actions in which to teach this man a lesson for such impertinence.

The more she thought over the conversation, the more furious she became. First Mrs. Hunter, then Captain Alexander, all trying to force their advice and their prejudices upon her.

There was excuse, Vivian thought, for Mrs. Hunter in that she was a withered and soured old woman who might have little understanding of modern youth and modern freedom, but from Captain Alexander it was unforgivable.

Only twice before had she met the man, on the first occasion of which she had done him a tremendous service.

Now not only was he ungrateful, but was presuming to criticize her actions as if he had some right to do so.

She drew a sheet of ship's note-paper towards her and wrote rapidly:

"I am looking forward to tonight. What time is dinner?" and signed it Vivian Carrow.

The steward brought her an answer ten minutes later. Vivian took the envelope from him and noticed that the paper was heavily monogrammed and of a superfine expensive quality.

In reality the pale-blue paper was a little vulgar, but at the moment Vivian was not in a mood to criticize the Prince, and she told herself that she liked a man who was fastidious in every detail.

"I shall be happy to welcome you at nine o'clock," the Prince had written in his own hand.

"So that is that," Vivian thought with a slight grimace which was meant for the discomfiture of Captain Alexander.

* * * *

Vivian surveyed her reflection in the mirror with satisfaction.

The white lace evening dress showed off her slim figure

64

to perfection and against it the two diamond clips which her father had given her as a birthday present glittered.

The dark waves of her hair were held in place by a tiny diamond star which had belonged to her mother.

In a mood of perversity she had taken more than usual trouble over her appearance this evening, feeling as she did so that it was in some way paying out Captain Alexander for his interference.

While she was dressing there came a knock at her cabin door, and when she opened it she found the Prince's native servant outside.

On the large silver salver which he held out to her lay a spray of white orchids flecked blood-red.

Vivian dismissed the man and then, alone in her cabin, gazed at the beauty of the flowers before she fixed them to her left shoulder.

They were only small blooms, and she guessed that they had been brought on board originally for the Prince's personal use and kept on ice so that he would be able to appear each day with a fresh flower in his buttonhole.

There was a luxurious extravagance in wearing English flowers fresh and unfaded when one was several weeks' journey from England.

Vivian felt that they added the finishing touch to her appearance; as she looked at herself she could not help wishing that Jimmy could see her.

Wouldn't he wish to recapture, if only for a short time, those moments when he had told her she was lovely, that her face fascinated him, and that she was the most beautiful girl he had ever seen?"

With a little shudder she thrust her thoughts from her. Jimmy must be forgotten.

She would concentrate on her feud with Captain Alexander and the adventurous and exciting future which lay before her.

Swiftly she turned towards the door, switching out the light in her cabin in passing, and with her head held high, she moved determinedly down corridors and companionways towards the Prince's suite.

She was ushered into the sitting-room by a turbaned native servant.

The moment she entered she was conscious of an almost overpowering fragrance of Eastern perfume. Sandalwood and musk mingled with some stronger and more exotic scent.

"His Highness will be with you in a moment," the servant said with a low bow.

In the moments that she was alone, Vivian had time to take stock of the cabin. The conventional painted walls and damask coverings had been curiously transformed.

The lights were lowered until they could only glow, soft-shaded and mysterious, on hangings of exotically embroidered silks.

Magnificent but somewhat barbaric ornaments of gold and silver held great bunches of flowers or were piled high with fruits or sweetmeats.

"How unlike anything I expected," Vivian thought to herself. "Fancy the Prince bothering to cart all this paraphernalia about with him."

She wondered if she might tease him about it, and yet she sensed that here in his own rooms she might meet a different personality from the European young man whom she had found such an agreeable companion these past weeks.

She was not to be disappointed. The door opened and the turbaned servant appeared bowing low, to be followed a moment later by his master.

"How lovely of you to come!" the Prince said conventionally.

His appearance made Vivian give a little gasp of surprise.

She had never seen him except in particularly stereotyped clothes from a Savile Row tailor, but tonight he wore a smoking suit of deep purple velvet, and in his buttonhole there was a companion orchid to those she wore on her shoulder.

It was not a particularly unorthodox dress, and yet somehow it altered his appearance.

There was a huge flashing diamond stud in his white shirt, and on his fingers for the first time since Vivian had known him he wore two rings, one a magnificent diamond set in gold and the other a carved cabochon emerald.

Even as the Prince took her hand in his Vivian found herself wishing swiftly that she had not come, and as dinner progressed she reiterated the wish again and again.

There was not only change in the Prince's appearance tonight, there was also a subtle alteration in his manner.

He drank very little and seemed only to toy with the richly spiced dishes which succeeded each other until Vivian felt that the dinner was never-ending.

His eyes, always black and compelling, were tonight queer and strange. The pupils were dilated until they appeared to Vivian to be abnormally large.

There was too a queer change in the Prince's speech, a slurring of syllables which Vivian had not noticed before in conversation with him.

An occasional mistake in grammar and English convinced her that he was not quite normal this evening.

She had seen men under the influence of drugs in China, yet she could not be sure that this was the explanation.

Perhaps, she told herself, he had enjoyed too many cocktails at the bar upstairs before coming down to dress.

She herself sipped champagne and talked disjointedly, conscious all the time that the Prince's eyes were fixed upon her.

At last the dinner was over, the serving tables were wheeled from the room, and the silently moving servants disappeared.

"Will you smoke one of my cigarettes?" the Prince asked Vivian, and because she was nervous she took one.

The Prince flashed an onyx and diamond lighter into life and held it towards her.

As she lit her cigarette she raised her eyes to his and, over the flickering little flame, she found him staring at her intently.

With a sudden touch of fear, she drew back and said quickly:

"What about the photographs you promised to show me of your father's palace? Don't forget that is what I have come to see."

The Prince clapped his hands and instantly the door opened and the servant stood waiting for orders.

The Prince spoke to him in Hindustani and, a moment later, the books were carried in. Laying them on a table, the servant waited and then, at a sharp command, disappeared again.

Vivian turned the pages, making conversation and forcing an interest in the hundreds of photographs of a palace which seemed to her a replica of every other potentate's residence she had ever seen.

Only a photograph of the Prince himself in full ceremonial dress really interested her. She looked at it for some time, making the usual commonplace remarks about the jewels and sword he wore.

"You like that photograph?" the Prince asked her.

"I think it is very good of you," Vivian replied. "Is that an emerald in your turban or a sapphire?"

"It is an emerald," the Prince answered. "But if you like the photograph I will give it to you."

He took the book from her hands and, roughly tearing out the page, pulled the surrounding photographs from it.

"Oh, please, don't spoil your book," Vivian said. "That is ridiculous."

"It is my pleasure to give you anything that you like," the Prince answered seriously.

"But I wish you had not done that."

She wondered what on earth she was going to do with the photograph now she had it.

"And in return," the Prince said, "you will give me a photograph of yourself?"

"That is impossible," Vivian replied. "I am never photographed. There is nothing I dislike more than posing in a studio, and snapshots are so unbecoming to me that I never keep them."

"Then it doesn't matter," the Prince said. "After all, how could I forget your face for an instant? It is always before my eyes."

"How awful for you," Vivian said lightly.

"You don't think that is true?" the Prince asked.

"Oh, of course I believe you, if you say so," Vivian said mockingly.

Then she added in an effort to change the conversation:

"What a lovely cushion that is on the sofa. Was it embroidered for you by the ladies in the palace?"

"I cannot remember," the Prince said, "but if you like it, it is yours."

"Oh no, really," Vivian said, protesting. "You cannot give me everything I talk about."

"And why not?" the Prince asked. "But I have here a present I wish you to have, a gift I want you to wear."

He took the large cabochon emerald from his finger and held it out towards her.

"No," Vivian said, rising to her feet. "It is awfully kind

68

and please don't think I am ungrateful, but I never accept presents from anyone."

"Perhaps not," the Prince said. "But from me, yes. I want you to have this, and please, you will take it."

He rose to his feet and walked a step towards her reaching out for her hand. Vivian backed a little away from him.

"No, really, " she said. "Don't let us have any argument. I have told you that I am very grateful for the thought but that I cannot accept such a present. Now let us be sensible and talk about something else."

"Why should we talk?" the Prince asked, his voice full of meaning.

Vivian moved a step backwards, her eyes on him.

"What about the records?" she said a little wildly. "You promised to play them to me."

"There is plenty of time for that," he replied, staring with his dilated eyes at her face.

He took another step towards her.

"You are very beautiful," he said hoarsely.

"If you are not going to play to me," Vivian said, doing her best to talk calmly, "I shall go away."

"Do you think I would let you go?" the Prince asked.

"I suggest you would be very silly to try to stop me," Vivian said, trying to speak with dignity.

The Prince came very near to her; he had only to put out his hand to touch her.

Yet he stood looking into her face, seeing the sudden fear in her eyes, which, however, proud and angry, defied him.

"You have come here to me," he said thickly, "and now I will not let you go."

He stood between her and the door. Vivian gave a little gasp and then she said in a voice cold, steady, and disdainful:

"You will kindly let me pass immediately. This joke has gone too far."

"It is no joke," the Prince replied.

Vivian was suddenly afraid to move. She knew without words, instinctively, that the Prince was only waiting, that at the slightest movement on her part he would put out his arms and hold her.

An agonizing fear gripped her. She knew that his last veneer of civilization was vanishing before her.

The Prince's expression had changed, and it was a beast who leered at her, waiting its time, choosing the moment in which to spring.

She felt her heart thumping, a dryness in her mouth, but she still held her chin high even while her breath came with difficulty and one hand strove to steady the tumult in her breast.

She faced the Prince, holding him, as it were, only by the defence of her eyes, yet all the time she was agonizingly afraid.

"If you scream, my pretty one," he said thickly, "no one will hear you. My servants are warned. We have all the night before us. Come to me willingly, come to me lovingly. I will hang you with pearls, I will give you all that you wish."

Through her fear Vivian felt a violent humiliation at his last words.

Was this all that it had meant, the companionship, the intellectual friendship she had offered him as they had sat hour after hour discussing things on the deck.

A woman to be bought, to be bribed with jewels, to be bargained for with finery.

"Let me go," she said.

Her voice was not angry or fearful, only bitter and ashamed.

The Prince laughed, and the sound was not pleasant. It held no mirth in its tones, it was only a cry of triumph. He put out his hands and she felt his touch on both her bare arms.

Vivian screamed, and even as she did so there came a loud knocking at the cabin door.

Neither she nor the Prince seemed to hear it, and then, suddenly alert as the knocking came again and again, he let go of her and turned towards the door.

"What is it?" he asked angrily.

At that moment there was a sound of voices raised in altercation with someone speaking loudly and commandingly in Hindustani.

Then, with a rattle and a crash, the door was forced open and, standing in the doorway with two Indian servants still protesting beside him, was Captain Alexander.

70

"What is the meaning of this?" the Prince asked furiously.

Captain Alexander scarcely glanced at him. He looked across the room to where Vivian was leaning weakly against the wall, her hands outstretched as if to support herself, her face very pale.

"Miss Carrow is wanted in the purser's office," Captain Alexander said.

He spoke quietly and yet with a note of command in his voice which somehow checked the angry words on the Prince's lips.

"Will you come at once?" he continued, addressing Vivian.

"Of course," she said.

But her voice was weak and seemed to come from her with an effort.

Slowly she walked across the cabin floor. As she reached Captain Alexander, he stood aside to let her pass, and the servants, still crowding the doorway, moved also.

Slowly and without a word Vivian and her escort left the cabin, neither so much as glancing towards the Prince, and he too was silent.

As they walked up the companionway which led to the deck Vivian stumbled and instantly a strong firm hand grasped her by the arm and held her up.

They went out on deck and there Vivian stood, gripping the handrail with both hands.

"I feel . . . faint," she murmured at last.

"I will go and get you some brandy," Captain Alexander said.

But instantly she turned to him almost hysterically.

"Don't go . . . don't leave . . . me . . . I can't be . . . alone."

"It is all right," he said quietly, speaking as he would to a frightened child. "Take your time, nothing can hurt you now."

They were on an unfrequented part of the deck. The only light was from the companionway behind them, casting a golden gleam which did not extend far into the darkness.

Vivian was breathing in gasps, fighting for control against the faintness and hysteria which she felt at any moment must overcome her.

Captain Alexander seemed to take little notice.

He too leaned against the rail, staring out to sea, and gradually Vivian became more reassured, her tense muscles relaxed and she smoothed back the hair from her forehead.

"How did you know?" she asked at last.

Her voice breaking the silence between them which had extended for over five minutes.

"Someone had to look after you," he said gently.

"God! How I hate men!" she said bitterly. "They are all the same."

"That is not true," Captain Alexander said softly.

"I loathe them," Vivian said wildly. "I loathe men, the world, and all that is in it. How I wish I were dead."

"Don't you think that is a little selfish?" came the quiet question from her side.

"Selfish to whom?" Vivian said. "My father cares for me but he is getting to be an old man. There is no one else, I haven't a single friend in the world, and anyone to whom I turn, to whom I offer my friendship becomes . . ."

Her voice broke and she could not finish the sentence.

It seemed to her that she was utterly isolated, utterly alone.

This evenings events had brought back overwhelmingly the misery and unhappiness she had felt just three weeks ago in Monte Carlo.

She had wanted to die then, but not more than she did now when this new humiliation had come upon her.

"Vivian," Captain Alexander said gently. "Will you marry me?"

Wildly she turned to face him.

"Is this a joke?" she asked.

She tried to speak severely, but her voice trembled on the words.

"Very far from it," he said evenly. "I want to marry you."

"I never want to marry anyone," Vivian answered fiercely. "And if I do, I promise it would not be you. I think perhaps I hate you."

"That is only because you don't know me as yet," he said.

"I know quite enough," Vivian said.

She spoke quickly, stung afresh by his conceit, by his confidence in himself.

"Perhaps you will think it over," Captain Alexander said very quietly.

"I shall think nothing over, and I regard it as an impertinence for you to ask me," Vivian replied hotly. "You are all I dislike, and you are also a murderer."

"That is not true," he said.

"I don't believe you," she said defiantly. "Circumstances are against you."

"Listen to me," Captain Alexander said.

He put his hands on her shoulders, turning her, so that she faced him in the darkness.

"One day I will make you believe it, just as one day I will make you love me."

"You are mad!" Vivian gasped. "I shall never love you."

It seemed to her that he suddenly grew bigger until he dwarfed her physically and mentally.

She could see by the light of the companionway a strange new glint in his deep-set eyes.

She found herself gasping for breath, for sanity and control, yet as though hypnotically influenced she could not tear her glance away from him.

It was as if deep waters were about to close over her head and drown her, and her consciousness would not let her go.

Again she heard his voice.

"And one day I will make you happy," he said very gently.

Then with a strange sound which was half a cry and half a groan, she slipped forward in a faint at his feet.

CHAPTER SEVEN

Speeding northward in the train from Calcutta, Vivian felt a sense of relief, of escape.

Strangely enough the person she most wished to escape from of all that boatload of people was not the Prince, but Captain Alexander.

Lying in her cabin where she had made herself a voluntary prisoner for the last few days of the voyage, she had considered the events which led up to her ill-fated dinner with the Prince.

She admitted honestly to herself that she was in a large part to blame for what had occurred.

While it did not alter her bitter and cynical emotions toward mankind as a whole, nevertheless she was prepared to acknowledge that she had behaved ill-advisedly, stupidly.

Disdain replaced Vivian's emotions of humiliation and anger where Prince Kowa was concerned, but toward Captain Alexander she felt more antagonistic than she had done hitherto.

His proposal of marriage, which had almost fantastically crowned the agitation and fears of the evening, had intensified her previous dislike of him ino a whole-hearted defiance and distrust.

Not for one moment could she imagine that he might be genuinely in love with her.

If he were, she told herself, it was certainly not the emotion as she knew or understood it.

Somehow it seemed an insult that this stranger, who had forced his way into her life, should offer her marriage when Jimmy had denied it her.

One evening Vivian crept up on deck at about one o'clock in the morning, hoping that everyone would be asleep.

She chose to walk along the upper deck and was thankfully feeling herself alone and unseen, when a movement

74

on the lower deck in a part reserved for third-class passengers attracted her attention.

To her surprise she saw there were several men down below and that they were standing in a circle around some object. Looking more closely she knew, even in the dim light, that the figure of one man with his back towards her was familiar.

As she wondered what Captain Alexander was doing at such an hour on that particular deck, she suddenly understood what was taking place.

A burial service was in progress.

She could just hear the murmur of the Captain's voice, and then, as the men bent down to raise the draped object which lay at their feet, Vivian, with a little gasp of horror, fled.

She could not bear to see the mortal remains of what had once been a passenger committed to the sea.

When she recalled his words: "One day I will make you believe it," she could not help but finish his sentence in her mind—"just as one day I will make you love me."

* * * *

It was a very pale Vivian who stepped out at Darjeeling. Her eyes deep-ringed from sleepless nights, her expression fretful from days and nights of worrying and turning over and over in her mind what had occurred.

She clung to her father with almost passionate fierceness when she found him duly installed in a small, unobtrusive hotel.

"The sea voyage doesn't seem to have done you much good," he said anxiously. "Do you think you are wise to come any further, my dear? Why not stay here and rest until I can return to you?"

Vivian smiled, a weary, rather bitter smile.

"If you only knew," she said, "how much I am looking forward to going to the forbidden land, to getting away from people, to escaping from those I most dislike and despise."

She spoke with such intensity that the Professor did not question any more but turned the conversation to plans for the future.

Vivian's first view of those amazing Himalayas was a little disappointing.

The densely covered mountains and the view of Darjeeling itself seemed to her at first to be merely a corner of Switzerland.

She asked herself why there was so much excitement about them and why she had expected something so very different.

Then a day came when her father took her out from the town and she saw the whole range of mountains spread out before her eyes, rising peak upon peak, the sun glinting on their snowy tips mounting into the clouds, dazzlingly erect, defying conquest, towering and impassable.

Then she knew that no words could ever describe the grandeur of the Himalayas, "Dwelling of Snows."

Some way up the mountain they could see the *stupas,* little square houses reached by perilous twisting mountain roads which the sure-footed native ponies traveled with equanimity.

For the first time Vivian felt really thrilled at what they were about to accomplish.

Behind those mountains lay a strange country and somehow, as she stared at the snows, she felt the future held out a promise of hope and of new courage even to her aching spirit.

But there was little time for introspection, or even for admiring the beauties of the mountains themselves.

Every morning weird pilgrims visited the hotel and conversed with the Professor and Vivian for many hours.

Used to picking up strange languages, they began to learn Tibetan with a will, only to find that a proficiency was not likely to be gained in years.

Even a smattering of the everyday phrases seemed to be a task requiring a concentration beyond Vivian's command.

Authorities on languages think it probable that at one time Tibetan was pronounced as it was spelled, but usage has rendered a great many of the letters silent and the majority of those composing a word are not pronounced at all.

To the uninitiated, therefore, the way a word is spelled gives no indication whatsoever of the way it is to be pronounced.

After every lesson Vivian felt herself grow more and more despondent of ever mastering a language which seemed to be as strange and unconventional as the country which produced it.

"One thing," she said laughingly to her father when they were alone, "I don't think you and I had better try and pass ourselves off as natives. I feel that we should be discovered the first time we opened our mouths."

"It is amazingly difficult," the Professor confessed. "I am beginning to find it easier to understand, but as a conversationalist I am afraid I shall never shine."

At last their plans were more or less shipshape, and then one day a strange but fine-looking man presented himself at their hotel.

His name was Surdar, and he informed the Professor that he had come to be his head servant on the journey which lay before them.

"Who sent you?" the Professor asked.

But Surdar, although he spoke and understood English, would not answer this first simple question.

"You go to Gyangtse," he said. "I, Surdar, will take you. I will find you boys and protect you."

"But who told you I was intending such a trip?" the Professor said in surprise.

So far in Darjeeling, he had not mentioned to a soul that he contemplated going any farther than into the interior of Sikkim.

"Surdar has come to be your head man," the Tibetan repeated steadily.

His recommendations were excellent, and he was by far the most efficient and suitable applicant the Professor had interviewed. He was engaged.

"Whether he has been sent by his own people," the Professor said to Vivian, "or whether he had some sort of supernatural instinct, of which one hears of so much up here, I do not know. Anyway, we can afford to take a chance. We shall be on the main trade route as soon as we pass through the Natu Pass."

Vivian had decided that to allay suspicion and to be quite certain that no one should anticipate that she was to accompany her father, she would travel down the line to the next station as herself.

Then she would catch the first train back to Darjeeling as the assistant in whose name the pass had been issued.

Accordingly, one fine morning, she kissed her father

goodbye on Darjeeling station, making a show of committing him to the care of Surdar, and waving farewell as the train moved out of the station.

She had a compartment to herself, and three hours later it was a dapper young man in his teens, wearing riding breeches, a battered panama, and dark sunglasses, who got out at a wayside station.

Vivian's hair had to be sacrificed to this disguise, but she had not cut it too short, allowing herself to look rather Byronesque.

She stained her face, neck and arms with diluted iodine and was surprised to see what an alteration it made to her appearance.

Certainly no one was likely to recognize her when she finally returned to Darjeeling, and the manageress of the hotel greeted her without any suspicion that only that morning she had been cooking her a substantial breakfast.

"Do you think I look all right?" she asked her father when they were alone.

"Perfectly," he said, looking her over critically. "But I should keep your glasses on, and I have arranged that we start tomorrow at dawn so there will be less likelihood of anyone talking to you. Thank goodness, tomorrow is Wednesday."

"Why?" Vivian asked. "I had forgotten it was, as a matter of fact, but what difference does it make?"

"Tuesdays, Thursdays, and Saturdays, according to the Tibetan religion, are bad days to start a new undertaking. Nothing would have induced Surdar and our native bearers to have moved unless their calculations assured them it was a propitious moment of the gods."

"How complicated," Vivian said lightly.

But she was to find herself for the next few months hedged about by far more annoying superstitions.

Her father had suggested that instead of taking a short cut to the pass which lies through the south of Sikkim, they should make a small detour.

They would thus avoid the possibility of meeting any Europeans or better-class travellers who would, of course, keep to the main roads.

On Wednesday morning Surdar had them safely en route.

The Professor, Vivian, and himself were mounted on

78

small ponies they had procured after much bargaining, and which were cheaper to purchase than horses.

The transport mules for the baggage were cheaper still, and these were piled high with baggage and led by three or four coolies who trudged along, singing joyfully in soft, rather melodious voices.

All along the paths, traders and pilgrims were wending their way, some riding wild white ponies, others on foot, intoning their prayers or murmuring with bent heads as they fingered rosaries of colored and carved beads.

It was a very early dawn, long before sunrise and the snows on the mountains were a soft iridescent amber.

A deep blue mist floated over the trees and hid the distance from view.

Vivian felt particularly light-hearted as they started on their way, their path lying first through the damp, hot, luxuriant forestland.

As soon as they had left the town the wild, almost barbaric beauty of the countryside began to reveal itself.

A soft chatter above her head made Vivian look up, and she had a fleeting glimpse of a small bearded monkey before it swung itself away from branch to branch.

Hovering overhead, seeking its breakfast, she could see a great eagle with wings outspread, somehow, in its lone but majestic flight, a perfect symbol of the mountains.

Almost immediately Surdar began to speak to her in his gentle voice, telling her legends and stories of the country through which they were passing.

The Professor called up one of the coolies and started to converse with him in Tibetan, but Vivian could not apply her mind this morning to lessons.

She wanted to begin to drink in some knowledge of the strange countries they were approaching.

First of Sikkim, which, though nominally independent, was still under British influence and control, and then of the 'Roof of the World,' Tibet itself.

The easy movement of her pony, the sweet, exotic smell of the land, the sharp tang of horseflesh and leather mingled with the beauty of the surroundings.

It seemed to Vivian that here, indeed, a new life was beginning to open in front of her.

When they reached an imposing-looking bridge which was, however, not completely secure they all dismounted.

Surdar insisted on this, and Vivian learned that it was not so much for safety's sake, but because to walk across a bridge is a sign of reverence to the gods of Tibet.

The bridge swayed dizzily and creaked ominously as they moved over it. In the centre Surdar paused, and drew from his pocket a bunch of little printed prayers in bright colored inks.

At the same time he told Vivian and the Professor to throw some copper coins, as an offering to the gods, into the water flowing swift and silver beneath them.

The coolies were chanting a prayer, and quite solemnly Vivian turned to do as she was told.

A sudden breath-taking view of the mountains made her stand entranced, a faint breeze rippling the sacred paper in her hands.

Then, following her father's example, she flung the little coin into the water and tied the paper prayer to the bridge, where it joined several others already there, somewhat weatherbeaten and tattered.

Bravely her little prayer fluttered out. It seemed to her bright, gay, and courageous.

It was with a sincere and humble supplication in her heart that she asked whatever gods there were to protect her in the unknown future.

"Help me," she prayed. "Bring me happiness."

Then the thought came to her like a voice:

"Could you be happy without love?"

* * * *

In Sikkim there are no great riches, but neither is there any poverty.

Over the hills, on which perch the little square-roofed monasteries, amid blossoming trees of peach and cherry, stand tiny white houses.

The peasants, their hats often entwined with wild flowers, pasture their cattle, till the soil, singing happily as they work, and smile shyly at any travelers they see on the narrow but well-kept roads.

Peach and cherry blossoms, orchids and wild peonies grow in profusion everywhere.

The orchids, of vivid exotic coloring, cling to the trunks of giant trees, and pink and purple, orange and scarlet azaleas cluster around them.

The snowy tips of the mountains were often hidden in

deep blue mist until suddenly the sun would strike through revealing an almost dazzling vision to the beholder.

It did not surprise Vivian that to the Buddhists this land was holy. From here their great Master started his mission, and it seemed to her impossible that evil or unkindness could exist in such a perfect land.

No wonder the people believed in reincarnation, no wonder they desired to live again amidst such beauty. Even the flowers seemed to be miraculous.

Surdar told Vivian of one precious plant, the black aconite, whose blossom lights up at night and by its glow can be found and picked.

He also told her of the Russian fire-flowers which are enchanted, and if found fulfill all wishes.

When night fell the little party would put up at a dak bungalow, one of the many charming little villas erected by the Indian Government solely for the use of travelers.

They are furnished, but every traveler brings his own bedclothes and his servants to look after him, although in attendance each bungalow has a *chowkidar* or caretaker.

Vivian and the Professor, after a long day's march, would sleep peacefully, and Vivian found that she was too tired to think.

All the hopelessness and misery of the past months were swept away from her by sheer physical exhaustion.

As soon as her bed had been made up she was only too glad to creep between the blankets and know nothing more until her father awakened her just before dawn.

Although both father and daughter were nervous little notice was taken of them once they had produced their passes.

They passed unnoticed through the town of Kalimpong, which has been called the 'Harbour of Tibet,' for it is where the Tibetans come to sell their goods and buy cheap knickknacks to barter in the markets at Lhasa.

Only one adventure altered for a short time Vivian's opinion of the country, which was when they stopped for lunch one day near the little village of Rango.

Surdar warned them that this part of Sikkim was noted as being dangerous for malaria and other fevers, and they took great care to boil their water and wrap themselves around in mosquito nets before they commenced to eat.

Vivian suddenly looked down to see a strange black animal on her arm.

With a little shudder she attempted to shake it off, but it was fixed firmly to the skin and only then did she realize that it was one of the most horrible creatures in the world, the Sikkim leech.

They travel along the ground like black earthworms and move by rising on their tails till they stand upright, then arching their heads down to the ground they bring their tails up to their heads.

Even with such a strange method of locomotion they move very quickly and scent animals and travellers a long way off.

Once they attach themselves to the human body, they suck the blood thirstily and it is impossible to tear them off without leaving a sore and dangerous wound.

Vivian screamed for Surdar who rushed up with a little bag filled with salt.

Dipping it in the river nearby he let the water trickle over the leech, which shrivelled up and fell away.

The ponies and mules had to be treated in the same way, for there was an innumerable quantity of these creatures which dropped down on the travellers from the bushes.

Vivian persuaded her father to hurry on and she only felt safe when they were many miles from the neighborhood of such pests.

At Gynagtok, the capital of Sikkim, no sooner had they arrived in the dak bungalow where they were to stay the night than six or seven servants arrived from the palace bringing presents of food and the compliments of the Maharajah.

The Professor returned the compliment by calling on the young ruler later in the evening, but Vivian stayed behind.

She was terrified that the Maharajah, who spoke excellent English, might be suspicious of her and think that she looked unlike the ordinary English young man.

The Professor returned filled with elation by the fact that the Maharajah had offered him, free of cost, some of his own mules and ponies to carry them to the great Tibetan outpost of Yatang.

This meant that they were likely to have no troubles at

the passes, and Surdar was overjoyed at the news, as the ponies they had brought from Darjeeling were already feeling the strain of the long marches.

"He was not suspicious of you at all?" Vivian asked.

"I do not think so," the Professor replied. "We discussed medicine at some length and the difficulties in this county of getting the peasants to use any form of modern sanitation or disinfectants.

"The Maharajah has very advanced ideas, but in such a land of legend, tradition, and superstition he finds it very difficult to make much progress."

"I wish I could have come with you," Vivian sighed. "I would have liked to see the palace."

"You would have been disappointed," her father answered. "For it is entirely European in style, although his wife came from Lhasa. Incidentally, his pet hobby is photography.

"He was very anxious to take a photograph of me, but I regretted that the light was not good enough tonight and that we should be leaving too early in the morning."

"That was wise of you," Vivian said. "One never knows what inquries he might be making."

"Alexander told me that he thought we need not worry until we get to the Tibetan frontier," the Professor replied.

"Do you think he knows?" Vivian asked casually. "Or was he just being reassuring?"

"Well, he has been through himself so often," the Professor answered, "that he ought to know the ropes."

"Oh!" Vivian said in surprise. "I did not know that he had been to Tibet."

"Of course he has," the Professor answered. "And I think he will be there when we arrive."

"Captain Alexander will be at Gyangtse?" Vivian said in horror. "Oh, Daddy, why didn't you say so?"

"I thought you realized that," the Professor answered. "Or did the Chief tell me after you had sailed? I cannot remember."

"But what will he say about me?" Vivian asked aghast.

The Professor shrugged his shoulders.

"My dear," he answered with a smile, "I thought of leaving you to cope with that situation. After all, once you are there, it will be very difficult for him to say anything."

After her father had left her and gone to his own

quarters for the night, Vivian lay awake staring into the darkness, a faint flush burning on her cheeks.

This was something she had not expected, to see Captain Alexander again so soon.

It was not the thought of him discovering how she had tricked the authorities and entered Tibet at her father's side which worried her.

It was the thought of meeting him after that last strange interview on board the ship.

He must have carried her down to her cabin, but when she recovered from her faint only the stewardess was with her giving her brandy and dabbing a handkerchief soaked with eau-de-cologne against her temples.

Strangely enough, the handkerchief was still with her, for some inertia had prevented her from returning it the following morning.

When she was packing at Darjeeling, she had found it among her things—of very soft white linen and in the corner the small embroidered initial—A.

"I wonder what his Christian name is?" she had thought.

Almost casually she had asked her father one day, when they were looking over some papers from the office in London and burning them.

"Alexander?" her father said absent-mindedly. "I have no idea, except that the Chief and other people in the office referred to him as Alec."

What should she say to him, and what indeed would he say to her? But as she pondered the problem, she fell asleep.

The three days' journey to the passes was to prove trying to the nerves of both men and beasts.

Vivian had a good head for heights but she felt sick and dizzy at times as the mule on which she was riding seemed to find a foothold on the very brink of nothingness.

She knew that one false step would dash her down the sharp rocks and impale her on the broken cragged stones below—the evidence of former avalanches.

On the last day the climb was so steep that it was impossible for her to ride and she had to walk roped to Surdar up some of the most precarious turns.

They were now nearly fourteen thousand feet up. The climbing was desperately fatiguing and the coolies began

84

to suffer from mountain sickness, and one of them began to bleed copiously at the nose and ears.

The Natu Pass was bleak, covered in snow, and a bitter wind swept through as if it wished to prevent them entering 'the Forbidden Land.'

Vivian was gasping for breath, her heart thumping, the blood throbbing in her temples.

When finally they reached the top, she had a view of the Tibetan empire, stretching away towards the sacred mountain of which they could just see the snowy summit.

Immediately below them lay the thickly-populated Chumbi Valley which they knew would lead them to the barren, desolate table-land of real Tibet.

As they reached the pass, Surdar shouted *"Lha-gyal-lo! Lha-gya-lo!"* which meant "Victory! Victory, to the Gods."

Each of them picked up a small stone to carry to the chorten where many travellers had laid tattered fragments of rags or paper prayers as a propitious offering to the Gods who had brought them safely through the pass.

When Vivian laid down her stone, keeping the sacred shrine to the right of her, she put out her hand and slipped it into her father's.

"Here begins our real adventure," she whispered.

* * * *

In the Chumbi Valley, Vivian saw her first Tibetans with the exception of the few traders she had met at Darjeeling and en route, and she was surprised by their beauty.

Tall, magnificently strong, and handsome, they were quite unlike what she had been expecting until Surdar told her that Chumbi is really quite distinct from Tibet, the people actually having a dialect and customs entirely their own.

As they approached the village of Yatang, the first thing they saw was a Union Jack flying over one of the houses.

The Professor, knowing this to be the British Agency, at once set off to call there and invite the help of the British Trade Agent to assist them with the frontier officials.

Mr. Williams was only too delighted to be of use, and it was lucky that he was with them, for the officials insisted on searching the Professor's luggage.

When they came to the portable cine-camera it looked as though things were likely to turn nasty.

"As a matter of fact, this is not for myself at all," the

Professor said to Mr. Williams. "I am taking it out at the express request of Mr. Andrews at Gyangtse."

"I am afraid they won't believe that," Mr. Williams said. "I think the best thing is for you to present it to the Abbot of the Chumbi monastery. He is well-known as a learned and brilliant man, and if you explain to the officials that this magic box is intended for him they may take it in good faith."

Although the Professor was upset at the loss of what he felt to be a valuable part of his equipment, there was nothing to be done but put a good face on the matter and do as he was told.

The officials were only partially satisfied at this explanation, but agreed on the condition that they should send one of the soldiers to accompany the Professor to the monastery first thing in the morning.

After much bowing and exchanging of compliments on both sides they were released and their passports stamped with the official stamp.

"That was a close shave," Vivian said to her father when they were alone.

He agreed but he still grumbled at the loss of his camera.

However, the next morning they set off and not far outside the town they came to the great Chumbi monastery.

Here they were received with great ceremony, with the roar of trumpets and conch shells, and the monks came down to the gate to meet them carrying fluttering prayer-flags in greeting.

They waited in the huge courtyard with its wide stone steps ascending to numerous buildings which were decorated with elaborate carvings, the roofs above gilded and peaked in Chinese style.

At one end of the courtyard, a party of lamas wearing flowing red robes were seated on the flagstones repeating in melodious tones prayers which were read aloud to them by an older man seated in their midst.

They took no notice of the visitors, seeming immersed in concentration.

After a short while the Professor and Vivian passed through the great Hall and were received in a smaller room by the Abbot's Chief Medical Teacher.

He was completely bald, but he had a heavy moustache, and his Buddhistic robe left one arm bare.

They sat down on the low couches while tea was brought to them in gold-encrusted cups made of green jade.

This was the first time that Vivian had tasted the Tibetan tea of which she had heard so much.

Her father had already instructed her that it is an insult not to drink and a still greater insult for the host to leave one's cup unfilled.

As soon as she had taken a sip her cup was filled again to the brim by a lama carrying a huge kettle.

The tea contained both butter and salt, and was rather like thick, not unpleasant soup.

Many compliments were exchanged on both sides, and then the old lama asked a question which Surdar translated.

"He says would you like to visit the Oracle? He is very famous and is the one who halfway through the great world war prophesied the exact month, day, and hour that the armistice would be declared."

"Oh, I would love to!" Vivian exclaimed at once.

They were led solemnly down the long silent passages until they came to the temple itself. Here it was very dark with an almost overpowering scent of incense.

Before great images burned the temple lamps lit by butter which flickered with a pure soft light.

It was all very silent and still, and then gradually as their eyes grew accustomed to the gloom they saw that at the far end, near the largest statue of all, was seated a strange man.

He was dressed in colored, brilliantly embroidered garments with a hat of gold and precious stones surmounted by feathers.

He held a sword and other strange objects in his hands, his eyes were shut, while his attendants, also wearing beautiful robes, knelt around him.

Led by the Chief Medical Teacher they drew nearer, and Vivian realized that the Oracle was in a trance, breathing deeply, moving his head from side to side all the while.

Every utterance he made was written down by one of the lamas, while the others repeated mandates of praise and adoration, bowing their heads to the ground or raising their arms in salutation.

"What would you like to ask?" Surdar whispered to Vivian.

"I do not know," she replied. "Has he anything to say to me?"

Surdar repeated her remark to the lama accompanying them, who, in his turn, murmured it to one of the officiating lamas who stepped down from the dais.

Taking Vivian's hand, he led her forward so that she stood a little in front of the others directly before the Oracle himself.

There was a moment's silence and then the Oracle moaned and groaned, turning his head from side to side while words poured from his mouth in a seemingly incoherent frenzy.

He spoke for perhaps two minutes and then relapsed into silence again.

Vivian bowed, and then they all crept quietly from the darkened temple to find themselves outside in the sunshine of the courtyard.

"What did he say?" she asked Surdar.

"He said," repeated the guide, "that you are not what you seem, that trouble will come to you but trouble will go away, that you must follow in the footsteps of the snow leopard if you would find life and love. You will be reincarnated many times but always for the better."

"What an extraordinary prophecy!" Vivian said lightly.

But secretly she was rather impressed that the Oracle had told her she 'was not what she seemed.'

"Don't you think he was good?" she asked her father later, when they had left the monastery.

"From what I know of oracles and fortune-tellers and prophets of all descriptions, their prophecies can be made to fit whatever happens. A small knowledge of psychology and a gift of observation can prove far more truthful when it comes to reading the future than half these so-called gifts of second sight."

"I think you are cynical," Vivian replied. "In my opinion, the Chumbi oracle was very good."

The Professor laughed.

"You wait till you get to the troubles," he said. "You won't be so keen to praise him then."

"You are a cynic," Vivian replied lightly. "And personally I don't think we are going to have any."

CHAPTER EIGHT

Jimmy held her tightly in his arms.

"I will make you love me!" he cried.

"But I do, I do!" Vivian replied, and then strangely his face changed, altered, and became the face of Captain Alexander.

She struggled and woke to find she had been dreaming and it was not human arms which held her but the blankets of her narrow sleeping-bag confining her limbs.

A shot rang out and then another, and with her heart beating wildly Vivian struggled to her feet and crawled to the tent opening.

Outside she could see by the light of the moon that her father was standing but a few feet away, firing at two men on horses who were galloping away, leading another riderless steed between them.

Surdar and the coolies came running up, shouting and calling.

Surdar fired also, but in a few minutes the horses and their riders had passed out of sight, disappearing into the barren sandy distance.

"What is the matter? Why are you shooting?" Vivian called, shivering a little in the bitter cold of the night wind.

"Robbers," her father said briefly. "They have taken one of our best horses, damn them!"

"What a country!" Vivian replied.

She looked out over mile after mile of even, monotonous

flat ground without a sign of scrub or human habitation.

In the daylight it was of one color, a dark and dirty yellow, the monotony of dry soil covered with sand and pebbles broken only by the beds of long-dried-up and forgotten rivers.

It seemed impossible that the occasional herds of antelope and wild asses, which scampered away at the approach of travellers, could find any form of sustenance.

Only the brilliant and dazzling snowy tips of the Himalayas which lay behind them recalled to Vivian and the Professor the beauties which now seemed like a forgotten dream.

They had been warned that robbers might be on the lookout for them should they choose to camp out rather than spend the night as was usual in the towns through which they passed.

But after one experience of the hospitality offered by the so-called inns Vivian had gone on strike and insisted that tents should be procured for their small caravan.

The first town they encountered ought to have warned them what to expect, for Pari is famed as the filthiest town in the whole world.

In the distance the town, which was protected by a great castle looked exceedingly beautiful. Near it was a tiny sacred island in the middle of a lake on which were erected thousands of prayer-flags.

As they came nearer, however, they discovered that its reputation was well deserved.

For years the refuse had been thrown into the streets until the level of the roads has risen so that they were the same height as the roofs of the houses, and Pari was literally buried in its own dirt.

Needless to say, Vivian and the Professor had not stopped there, but had travelled on until they found what appeared to be a small but clean town. They were, however, too optimistic.

When they arrived they were greeted effusively by the Nemo, or landlord.

Tibetan houses are built more or less on the same plan. They are nearly all two or three stories high and built around a courtyard on which verandas look from the first and second floors, communicating one to another by an outside staircase.

As the courtyard was used as a depository for refuse of all kinds, it was not surprising that the ground floors were used only for stables or warehouses and occasionally for servants' quarters.

The master of the house slept on the top floor as it would be beneath his dignity to have the feet of an inferior being or servant over his head.

Vivian and the Professor were shown into a large empty room as all travellers, brought they own bedding and cooking utensils—a wise precaution from a sanitary point of view, if from no other.

They had, however, to share the fire of the household, and here Vivian for the first time encountered the acid smoke of yak dung which is used as fuel all over Tibet.

It made her eyes smart and burn and its dry rather bitter taste seemed to linger afterwards in everything she ate.

Around the fire when they entered the living room were seated five or six men, four of whom, Surdar informed Vivian, were husbands of the landlady.

Polyandry was practiced throughout Tibet and a woman who marries was automatically the bride of all her husband's brothers.

Looking at their hostess in her voluminous dress of many colors, with her dark hair piled high on her head, ornamented with an immense head-dress of coral and turquoise, Vivian was struck by her dirtiness.

She was to learn later that not only was this considered a virtue in the eyes of the Gods, but also a protection against the bitter winds and the innumerable lice which infected most Tibetan houses.

"Even in the interest of adventure and new experiences, darling," she said to her father next morning, "I refuse to spend another night in a Tibetan house."

"I rather agree with you," the Professor said gloomily, for he himself had not passed unmolested.

Luckily their equipment included a tent for themselves, and for the servants they were able to procure one made of black yakskin, the sort usually used by the nomads or herdsmen who moved about with their cattle over the countryside.

The Professor was all the more inclined to camp out

as the coolies had spent the evening drinking *arak,* the most intoxicating drink in Tibet.

It was so potent that two or three of the coolies had come to blows and were certainly in no fit state the following morning for a long day's march.

Surdar, however, fell upon them with curses and blows, which they took in a philosophical manner, being apparently used to that kind of treatment.

But they lagged behind during the whole day's journey and arrived at the final camping-place long after the others had settled down and commenced their night meal.

Surdar became very nervous as they neared this well-known spot.

"It is noted for its bandits and highwaymen," he told Vivian. "Perhaps those who visited us the other night already carried the news that we have good mules and good money with us."

Vivian looked ahead to where the steep rocks seemed to bend into a natural trap for unwary travellers like themselves.

"Can't we get protection of any sort?" she asked.

"I have already prayed to the Gods," Surdar answered her seriously.

"Effective as Surdar's gods may be," Vivian said humorously to her father, "a couple of stalwart soldiers would be more reassuring."

"We must just hope for the best," the Professor said philosophically, taking out his revolver and seeing that it was loaded.

Slowly they descended into the gorge, apprehensively glancing to right and left.

Everyone's nerves were slightly on edge, for fear is perhaps the most insidious and quite the easiest emotion to excite the human breast.

Suddenly behind some rocks Vivian saw a movement and a moment later five horsemen came into view.

One of the coolies let out a yell of fright, but the horsemen made no movement, obviously waiting for the small party to draw abreast of them.

"What are we going to do?" Vivian asked anxiously.

The Professor pondered for a moment and then he handed her the second revolver that he carried.

"When I say 'Go!'," he said, "fire three shots quickly into the air. I think it is our one hope."

Slowly they plodded on, and then when they were about fifty yards from the horsemen, who all carried rifles, the Professor waved his revolver in the air and shouted "Go!"

He and Vivian fired simultaneously, and the repercussions echoed and re-echoed round the gorge until the noise was almost deafening.

With one accord the five horsemen turned and galloped away, followed by the laughter and shouts of the coolies and some very rude remarks from Surdar which Vivian could not understand.

That night they camped on the plain on to which the narrow valley admitted them.

Ahead of them they could see the town of Gyangtse, their goal built on the side of a small turreting hill surmounted by a castle, while in the distance snow-capped mountains encircled the plain.

What lay before Vivian was immaterial.

Even her apprehension at meeting Captain Alexander paled before her triumph at what she had already achieved.

She was one hundred and fifty miles inside the frontier, undetected in her disguise, and so far undefeated by all the hardships of the journey.

Nearer and nearer they drew until the town with its flat roofs seemed almost insignificant and dwarfed by the high and very beautiful castle which looked as fine as some of those on the Rhine as it towered on the pointed yellow hill.

"It is the most beautiful in all Tibet," Surdar assured Vivian. "The foreign devils destroyed it, but the Gods have commanded and it has been rebuilt again."

Vivian knew that the foreign devils he referred to were the Younghusband Expedition of 1904.

However, she left his observation pass and, pointing to a strong sturdy-looking bulding about a mile and a half away from the castle and some way up the hill, she inquired what that was.

"That is where the English soldiers live," Surdar replied.

At his words Vivian spurred her horse forward and drew abreast of her father who was riding in front lost in contemplation.

"Look!" she said, pointing with outstretched hand. "Look, Daddy, there is our destination. We have done it, and now, come what may!"

The Professor smiled at the joyousness of her tones, and, with smiling faces, they rode on towards Gyangtse.

* * * *

"This is most irregular," Mr. Andrews, the British trade agent, had said when Vivian had explained who she was.

He had scratched his grey head reflectively, but his eyes had twinkled, and she had felt that there was little to fear from him at any rate.

"I do not know what the authorities are going to say," he went on.

"Must you tell them?" Vivian asked.

"I am afraid I shall have to," he answered. "But I think that this calls for writing a careful and diplomatic letter. In other words, it will take some time, Miss Carrow, and meanwhile you can do what you like."

"You are an angel!" Vivian said impulsively.

"Of course, there is a telegraph-wire from here to Kalimpong," he said, but laughed when she answered:

"Forget it!"

They were all seated comfortably around the table after dinner the first good meal Vivian had enjoyed for many days, and she had eaten until she assured Mr. Andrews she could manage no more.

"All the same," he said seriously, "I think I should wear riding-breeches and your dark glasses when you move about in the town itself. You will be less conspicuous that way. The Tibetans seldom see a woman of any other nationality and you don't want to be mobbed. It is no pleasant experience, I can assure you."

"I think it is the pluckiest thing I ever heard," a voice said frankly from the other end of the table.

Vivian smiled as she met the admiring eyes of Tony Grayling, the young lieutenant in charge of the soldiers billeted in Gyangtse.

Tall and fair, with the fresh complexion of an English schoolboy, he was apparently quite unaffected so far by the extremes of the Tibetan climate.

He was also obviously thrilled to meet a white woman after six months in what he termed "the back of beyond."

"Thank heavens we can manage a bridge of four," he

told Vivian seriously, later in the evening. "That is, when the Doctor is here. He has charge of both this place and Yatang and spends his time traveling between the two. My captain, who makes the fourth, is at present home on sick leave, so Andrews and I have had a pretty dull time of it playing picquet."

"Don't you ever have any other excitement?" Vivian asked.

"As far as I can make out," Tony answered in contempt, "nothing happens here from one year's end to another. Luckily, we only have a year's service here, otherwise I think I should become a lunatic and they would find me with straws in my hair believing I was a local god or something."

"That reminds me," Vivian said. "I would like to see the monastery and the temple. Will that be possible?"

"Rather!" Tony answered enthusiastically. "I will take you myself."

"Do you think you will be an experienced guide?" Vivian asked.

"I must admit I have only been there once," he answered. "But we will find you someone who knows all about it, if that is possible."

"Is there no one else English here?" Vivian asked casually. "We were told that a Captain Alexander would meet us."

"Oh, Alec!" Tony said. "He pops in and out. I don't know when he is expected back."

"Pops in and out?" Vivian queried. "What do you mean by that?"

Tony went rather pink in the face and spoke slowly, obviously choosing his words.

"Well," he said reflectively, "he has various places and things to see to round about here. Administrative jobs, you know."

Vivian laughed.

"You needn't be so secretive with me," she said. "I suppose you mean he is doing a bit of spying and you don't like to say so."

"I can't discuss Alec, Miss Carrow," Tony said, not meeting her eyes.

"Orders are orders, I suppose," Vivian replied.

"Exactly!" Tony answered.

Vivian liked him for his adherence to duty in spite of what she knew must be a temptation to talk frankly with her.

"I suppose Mr. Andrews knows why you have come here?" she said to her father.

They were alone in the small but comfortable sitting room which had been allocated them and from which they had a magnificent view overlooking the town and the plain beyond.

"Of course he does," the Professor replied. "But he knows very little himself. So far as I can make out we are to wait until Alexander returns. In the meantime, I shall get to know the town, and the environments of Gyangtse as far as I am allowed to.

"I have already suggested that we should ride in the morning. We English must have our exercise, you know, and the Kenchung, who seems to be the local authority, has given us permission to go anywhere within certain specified boundaries."

"Well, that is one step in the right direction," Vivian answered. "Did you speak to him in his own language?"

"Of course I did not," the Professor replied. "I made it quite clear that neither of us understood one word of Tibetan and had no interest in trying to. In fact I was exceedingly insular and informed him through an interpreter that I had no desire to do anything but enjoy a peaceful if energetic holiday."

"I hope he believed you," Vivian said.

But there seemed little reason to doubt that the Professor had been entirely convincing when the following morning they were allowed to exercise their horses several miles beyond the town.

Once out of sight the Professor drew glasses from his pocket and examined searchingly the distant hills.

"That is the pass which Andrews believes one can get through, though it is seldom used," he said, turning to his daughter and handing her the glasses.

"If I can get through there," the Professor went on, "making out as an excuse that I was lost, I can do several days' surveying of the surrounding country before meeting a search party sent out anxiously by you and Andrews to meet me on the main Lhasa route which lies to the right."

"It sounds all right," Vivian said. "Will Surdar go with you?"

"I hope so," the Professor replied. "I think he is entirely trustworthy, although I still haven't fathomed the mystery of his arrival. Anyway, I shall do nothing until Alexander arrives. Andrews expects him very shortly."

Vivian by now had steeled herself to the point of almost wishing to meet Captain Alexander and get it over.

Her half-formed wish was to be granted sooner than she expected, for when they returned home to lunch after their ride it was to find him standing in the sitting room of the Block House.

"How are you, Professor?" he said gaily, holding out his hand.

Then turning to Vivian he shook hands without speaking.

"Are you surprised to see me?" Vivian inquired.

She was half nervous, half irritated at his lack of astonishment at her presence.

Captain Alexander smiled in the faintly superior way Vivian most disliked.

"I knew the day you left Darjeeling," he said quietly.

"I wonder you did not try to stop me," she said almost heatedly.

She wondered why this man had the power to drive her to fury by whatever he said or did.

"Why should I spoil such a very pleasant addition to the party?" he asked.

Before she could find words in which to answer him luncheon was announced.

Captain Alexander spoke very little during the meal that followed, and Vivian, feeling the old antagonism rising in her, turned her attentions to Tony.

She was only too glad to chatter away, talking absurdities with a zest and enthusiasm which made the meal pass swiftly and amusingly.

"Are you coming up to the monastery this afternoon, Miss Carrow?" he asked as they finished.

"But of course," Vivian replied. "We arranged that, didn't we?"

"If you don't mind, Tony," Captain Alexander said quietly from his end of the table, "I should like to take Miss Carrow there myself. There are one or two things I particularly want to show her."

There was disappointment in the boy's face, but he answered at once:

"Of course, Alec."

He looked towards the elder man with such youthful adoration and admiration that Vivian somehow checked the words of protest that had risen on her lips.

She would not draw Tony, she thought, into the friction between herself and Captain Alexander.

Yet she was annoyed and felt that she would pay him out by being as cold and distant as possible however interesting the afternoon should prove.

But her attitude was to be a difficult one to maintain.

As they rode from the Block House, down towards the marketplace which belonged, as did a large section of the residential portion of the city, to the monastery, Captain Alexander said:

"Don't be cross, Vivian. There are such a lot of really interesting things I want to show you this afternoon.

For a moment she wanted to defy him.

Then she was aware that he could tell her so much she wanted to know, so instead of protesting further she replied with a half hesitating smile:

"Very well, Alec."

They did not speak again until they had passed through the marketplace and were rising toward the monastery built on the slope of the hill above the northern part of the town.

Then as the horses took their time, for the ascent was steep, Alec looked towards Vivian and put out his hand.

"Will you be friends?" he asked.

Vivian felt the warm blood rushing into her cheeks.

She had not expected this from him and impulsively she held out her ungloved hand and laid it in his.

As he held it firmly in his grasp she felt a sudden fear of his strength, of his strangeness, of something unknowable about him.

Then she answered steadily, stressing the word, "Yes, *friends,* of course," and again in silence they rode on towards the monastery.

They were met by a bowing lama, and after they had taken tea with the Abbot in his own private rooms they were shown round the building.

The Gyangtse Monastery was not particularly large, but

it had a historical interest, and was considered important by the authorities at Lhasa.

From thousands of miles the Tibetans came on a pilgrimage to the Golden Pagoda, the great golden shrine whose cone-shaped roof Vivian had noticed as she approached the monastery.

Let into the walls at the base of the pagoda were numbers of revolving prayer-wheels.

The pilgrims turned the wheels, and with every revolution they believed they were rid of many sins and saved themselves from many rebirths.

"This is what I want you particularly to see," Alec said.

He led Vivian through the great Du-Kang or hall and on to a small chapel on the third story of the monastery which was known as the Hall of the Abbots.

All around the walls were images representing the archbishops of the past.

They wore curious mitres and ceremonial robes, and Vivian stared at them for some time without noticing anything very peculiar and then she exclaimed:

"Why, they might belong to some Catholic Cathedral in France or England. They don't look as if they were Tibetans at all."

"Exactly!" Alec said. "That is what I wanted you to notice, and that is one of the strangest things about this country."

"What do you mean?" Vivian asked with interest.

Their lama guide was praying in a corner of the chapel and Alec moved until they were out of earshot, though it was unlikely that he could understand English.

"I believe," Alec said, "that the intellectuals of ancient Tibet, to whom we owe the great Yoga philosophy, were in fact the founders of the Aryan race."

"But is it possible?" Vivian asked.

"Quite," Alec answered. "And every day we discover more and more proofs that this is so. Look at the aquiline noses of these abbots, for instance. Are they not an amazing contrast to the broad flat features of the peasants you see everywhere or even the lamas themselves? But I will show you something even more amazing."

He drew her into the temple, past the two fearsome images at the entrance hall which the Tibetans believed prevent evil spirits from entering the temple to tempt the monks from their prayers.

Inside it was very still and quiet, only the flickering butter lamps revealed the sweet meditative face of the Buddha enshrined in gold and precious stones. But Alec led the way to another image.

"This," he said, "is 'The Buddha who is to Come,' the next master destined to be born into the world and to whom every good Buddhist already prays that his advent may be soon and that he may bring peace to us all."

Vivian looked up at the huge god towering above them and then gave a gasp of surprise, for instead of sitting cross-legged in an Oriental attitude the Maitreya was shown sitting on a chair in European fashion.

His garments were of gold and precious stones, but his skin was nearly white and the eyes, downcast in meditative contemplation seemed to hold a touch of blue.

"A European," Vivian said. "It is extraordinary."

"Perhaps the prophecies will come true," Alec said. "Perhaps a great teacher will arise in the West. Who knows?"

* * * *

"But I thought," Vivian said later, as they left the monastery on the hill behind them and moved slowly down the worn mule track toward the sunlit plain, "that it was the monks you were frightened of around here."

"Oh, not in this monastery," Alec replied. "The one of which we have had such bad reports is the monastery of Kun-wa-pa. Perhaps I had better explain to you. The Lamas of Tibet are divided into two classes known as Red Hats and Yellow Hats.

"The Yellow Hats are Buddhists and are the best and also the highest, but the Red Hats who are of a lower status altogether are sometimes known as the fighting monks.

"What is more serious is that their faith is really based on the old Bon-po or black faith, which existed long before Buddhism was adopted by the country.

"The Bon-po is a religion of sorcery and magic. They are bad with the diabolical wickedness of people who have strange powers, added to which they are hostile to the Buddhists.

"A few years ago we believed that Bon-po had died

out of the country or was practiced by a few isolated secret sects, but now it has begun to grow again.

"The Tantrik lamas not only prey on the superstitious and fearful minds of the peasants, but undoubtedly also have some form of devilish power which makes them terrifying as well as dangerous from anyone's point of view."

"Do you mean," Vivian said incredulously," that you believe in black magic and all that sort of thing?"

"When you have lived in this country as long as I have," Alec replied, "you will know that one is bound to believe, however fantastic it sounds."

"And so it is the monks of Kun-wa-pa whom you imagine are in league with the Russian Syndicate?" Vivian said.

Alec nodded.

"I am afraid so," he replied. "They are greedy for money, as long as they can grasp it by any means which does not entail work or trouble for themselves. Only last night one of our men brought us most disquieting news.

"Tomorrow your father starts off on his first effort of exploration beyond the mountains. I want you to go riding, to move about the town quite unconcerned until at least twenty-four hours have passed.

"Then we will begin to appear agitated, and finally we must report that he has lost his way to the Kenchung.

"You will be worried, thinking that he must have had some small accident of sorts."

"He will be all right?" Vivian asked anxiously. "There is no real danger?"

"So far as I know, none," Alec replied. "Our plans are all cut and dried. On the third day the search party will find him, wandering lost and bewildered on the Lhasa road.

"His servants will be cursed, but after all they came from Sikkim and are not supposed to be any wiser than their master."

"It sounds all right," Vivian said doubtfully. "I suppose you would not let me accompany him?"

"I think it would be most unwise," Alec replied. "The idea is he goes off for a ride accompanied by only one servant.

"The afternoon winds and early nightfall lead them out of their road and they wander, lost and miseable, over the plain.

101

"In actual fact they will make straight for the pass in the mountains and strike off in the direction that we most want surveyed."

A sudden scream interrupted their conversation.

As they turned the corner into one of the narrow dirty streets they saw a large man brandishing a long whip of yakhide and rushing after an undersized, ragged coolie boy.

As they watched the boy was caught and the man started to belabor him over the head and shoulders with the whip, striking again and again while the victim shrieked in undisguised agony.

"A thief, I should imagine," Alec said briefly.

He turned his horse toward a side street so as to avoid passing the struggling pair, but Vivian was suddenly incensed by such brutality.

The heavy whip had already broken the skin on the coolie's face and blood was streaming from the wound. The large man, however, seemed to have no thought of stopping the barbaric punishment he was meting out to his victim.

Again and again he struck, until the coolie, little more than a child, was forced on his knees, still uttering desperate cries for help and striving to keep off the blows with supplicating quivering hands.

Without a moment's thought, Vivian urged her horse forward until she was beside the striker.

"Stop that! Stop that!" she said, speaking in English, but there was no mistaking the tone of her voice.

In surprise the bully did stop, his arm arrested as he was about to strike, and without a moment's hesitation the coolie slipped from his grasp and rushed down the street and away.

"How dare you be so cruel?" Vivian said severely.

The Tibetan let forth a flow of violent aggressive language and then spat forcibly towards her even as she turned her horse.

Then, as if further incensed by her attitude of disdain and indignation, he raised his whip and flicked the long curling lash at her just as she moved off.

Vivian, taken off her guard, ducked so that the whip missed her, but in the swiftness of her action her hat fell from her head and rolled onto the cobbled street.

At that moment Alec came riding up and dismounting returned her hat, at the same time speaking in stern Tibetan to the man who stood defiantly, arms akimbo, in the center of the road.

The man answered sullenly and abruptly, and then pointing a finger at Vivian let forth a stream of unintelligible but obviously bitter and virulent language.

Vivian took no notice, but thanking Alec for her hat she replaced it on her head and then, without looking around, they rode slowly down the street.

The voice of the angry man followed them until they had turned the corner and gone some distance on their way to the Block House.

"What was he saying?" Vivian said, when they were out of earshot.

"It was a very unwise thing for you do do," Alec said sharply. "You must be mad to interfere in a local brawl."

"If you can stand by and see such brutality," Vivian replied, "I can't."

All her former antagonism was rising again at the dictatorial note in Alec's voice.

"The point is that you are not in a position to interfere," he said severely.

"Well, I can't see that it matters," she said, uneasily aware that there was reason in what he said.

"One never knows," he replied, speaking almost as if to himself.

"Was that man cursing me?" Vivian asked a moment or so later, out of curiosity.

"He was," Alec replied grimly.

"Oh well," Vivian replied frivolously, "we will see which is stronger, the curse of a Tibetan peasant or my very twentieth-century scepticism."

"Unfortunately, the man is not a Tibetan peasant," Alec replied.

"How do you know?" Vivian asked. "Have you seen him before?"

"Never," Alec answered, as they reached the Block House and passed through the sentry-guarded gateway.

"Well, then, who is he?" Vivian asked agressively.

"A lama of the Red Hat faith," Alec said abruptly.

Although she told herself it was absurd, she felt a little throb of fear.

CHAPTER NINE

Tony Grayling was a very normal and a very charming young man.

His heart was very elastic and he gave it plenty of scope by proceeding to fall in love with almost every attractive young woman he met.

Needless to say, from the first moment that he set eyes on Vivian he 'fell for her,' as he himself naively put it, 'head over heels.'

Vivian was amused, and she found his obvious admiration and adoration made the passage of the days easy and entertaining.

There was no desperate heart-tearing emotion, or any subtle complexity of sex or mind. It was just natural, human, and enjoyable.

Love to Tony was simple and inevitable and his undisguised pleasure in her company helped, perhaps, more than anything in healing that still throbbing wound to Vivian's pride.

While Alec seemed more and more aloof and detached from the party, Tony and Vivian found no lack of interest in each other or in their absurd and sometimes childish ways of passing the hours between meals.

Even Vivian, however, flushed slightly when Alec, striding unexpectedly into the room with orders for Tony found them sitting on the floor building card castles.

"Look out! Don't make a draft!" Vivian said as he entered, thinking it was her father.

Then as Tony asked, "Do you want me, Alec?" She realized who stood behind her.

She slowly turned her head to face Alec, a faint color rising to her cheeks.

Tony took the papers Alec held out to him, listened carefully to his instructions, and then hurried off, saying to Vivian before he went:

"I shall only be an hour or so. Don't forget you have promised me my revenge at six-pack Bezique."

As the door slammed behind him Vivian got up from the floor, shaking the creases out of her green skirt.

There was a little silence, but intuitively, although she did not look at Alec, she felt that his eyes were on her.

After a moment she felt the silence to be oppressive, pregnant with deep meaning, and hastily, almost nervously, she started to speak.

"Is Daddy fretting?" she said lightly. "How much longer do you think the storm is going to continue? It is no use him going until it has completely died down, he would be frozen to death if he had to stop all night on the mountains now, wouldn't he?"

Alec brushed her words aside, and, fixing his eyes on her half averted face, he asked very softly:

"Why are you avoiding me, Vivian?"

"Avoiding you?" Vivian echoed in insincere surprise. "I assure you I am doing nothing of the sort. After all, it would be rather difficult in such cramped quarters, even if I wanted to."

"Vivian," Alec said, taking a step forward, and his voice vibrated on her name, "look at me."

Almost fearfully Vivian obeyed, raising her head until, nearly on a level with his, their eyes met and he held her glance almost, it seemed against her will.

There was something inscrutable, something she half feared, in his expression, and yet she had to look at him and she found herself murmuring almost inaudibly:

"What do you want me to do?"

She trembled when she had spoken, and then gravely his voice, just audible to her hearing, answered:

"I want you to learn to love me."

He did not touch her, he did not come any nearer, and yet she felt that he held her in such a close embrace that she could not escape.

She stood looking at him breathlessly, a strange unaccountable sensation quivering in her throat.

Then with a little gasp and a sudden almost violent effort, she turned from him and ran across the room.

She opened the door and only then did conversation make her pause and say:

"I've got to change my clothes. I shall see you at tea, shan't I?"

She tried to speak naturally, but her voice broke on the commonplace words, and she dared not look at the man standing so still and so silent in the center of the room.

"Why am I such a fool?" Vivian asked herself fiercely when she reached her bedroom. "What is there about Alec which frightens me? It is ridiculous. I have never been afraid of anyone before."

Those were the only few moments that they had alone during the next two days and Vivian was thankful that the attentive Tony made any *tête-à-tête* impossible.

In fact, she clung to the protection of his presence, making him always the object of her conversation.

Only on the fifth day of their enforced imprisonment, when Tony tried to kiss her as she was going up to bed, did she wonder if she was perhaps being unwise and unkind, in encouraging the attentions of the young man.

"Don't be ridiculous, Tony!" she said, as he put his arm around her.

"You are quite divine," he told her. "Kiss me good night, Vivian."

"I shall do nothing of the sort," she said, speaking severely, at the same time laughing.

"Don't be so mean to me, darling," he pleaded. "It is such heaven having you here; and I adore you, you know that."

He looked so like a small boy pleading for an extra chocolate that Vivian had to laugh.

"Don't be silly," she said. "What about all the lovely creatures at home who are kissing your photograph good night and sleeping with it under their pillows?"

"What the eye doesn't see, the heart doesn't grieve after," Tony quoted with a grin.

Then before Vivian could stop him he kissed her cheek.

"Will you behave!" she said, stamping her foot and trying to sound really angry.

"But I am," he said in astonishment. "You ought to be delighted with me really."

."Go to bed at once," she commanded, "or I shall scream for protection."

"All right," he said. "But as a lesson I shall carry you to your bed first."

And in spite of her protests he bent down and picked her up in his strong arms.

"Don't be so absurd, Tony," Vivian protested, trying to struggle and yet laughing at the same time.

They were making more noise than they knew and at that moment Alec opened his bedroom door and looked out at them.

"What is all this?" he started to say.

In the dim light, he stood looking at the embarrassed and slightly ruffled Vivian, although she did not know if there was disapproval or disgust in his inscrutable expression.

"It's all right, Alec," Tony said cheerfully. "I was just showing a little hospitality to our fair guest."

With that he carried the still struggling Vivian into her room and bounced her down on the small bedstead.

"I am furious with you," she started to say, but without waiting for further comment, Tony blew her a cheery kiss from the door and disappeared.

But it was not of him and his blue eyes that Vivian was thinking a moment later as she lay where he had put her on the Chinese embroidered cover of her bed.

Was Alec horrified at her, she wondered. Did he think she was incapable of being with any man without indulging in some form of flirtation?

Always he seemed to come upon her at her worst moments.

Ragging with Tony could hardly compare with her misery in the summerhouse or her scene with Prince Kowa, and yet Alec must invariably appear when she was at a disadvantage.

Again she told herself that she hated him, and yet her last thoughts were of him that night before she sank into a dreamless sleep.

Vivian was still sleeping when a knock at her door startled her into wakefulness.

"What is it?" she called, and a moment later her father entered.

"I am just off, my dear," he said.

"Is it fine?" she questioned.

He threw open the shutters which barred her small

window and the sunlit plain beneath was sufficient answer to her question.

"Take care of yourself," she said anxiously.

"Of course," he smiled. "Don't worry. There is absolutely no danger. Even if I am caught and prevented from doing my work, I shall only be brought back here to be judged by the Ken-chung."

"But I hope you are successful," Vivian said, "and then I shall have some work to do. I certainly haven't earned my keep up to now."

The Professor patted her shoulder affectionately.

"I wouldn't have come without you for anything in the world," he said.

"Thank you, darling," Vivian replied holding out her arms. "God bless you, and the very best of luck. I shall be praying for you."

"Don't break too many hearts while I am gone," the Professor said with a whimsical smile, "and for goodness sake don't get mixed up in local rows."

"So Alec told you," Vivian said.

"Yes," her father replied. "He is rather worried about it. The people are naturally of a sullen and resentful temperament, so one never knows what far-reaching results some obscure and unimportant action may have."

"Oh, Alec's an old woman," Vivian said crossly.

"On the contrary," the Professor said seriously. "I consider him one of the most brilliant young men I have ever met."

"Brilliant?" Vivian questioned with raised eyebrows.

"Brilliant and sensible," the Professor said, "and I would rely on his judgment. Incidentally, I have left you in his charge and as his special care while I am gone."

As Vivian did not speak, struck into sudden silence by his last observation, he added:

"I must be off."

Again he kissed her tenderly and then, almost before she could realize it, she could hear the distant voices and noise of his departure.

When she came down to breakfast nearly an hour later, it was to find Tony and Alec had already finished and Mr. Andrews was her only companion.

"Any news?" she asked him.

"Not much," he replied. "There are some disturbing reports from the North, on the Russian border, but one cannot believe them. More lies are invented in this country than in any other place in the world, and yet one never knows."

Moodily he poured himself out another cup of tea.

"Aren't you getting sick of the food?" he asked.

"Not much variety in it, is there?" Vivian said.

"It is infuriating to think," Mr. Andrews grumbled, "that the rivers further on in the country are packed with fish, but it is almost impossible to arrange for the proper transport of them even providing we could get someone to catch them. These damn fools won't eat them, just as they consider chicken as unclean."

"But I have always been told," Vivian said, "that Tibetans adore eggs, having learned to enjoy them from the Chinese."

"Oh they do," Mr. Andrews replied, "but only so old that they are quite uneatable from our point of view; and it is no use asking the peasants to bring you fresh eggs. They simply don't understand the word.

"Two or three months old is a fresh egg to them, as opposed to the five or ten years of what they think is a decently eatable one. Hence my difficulties."

Mr. Andrews ruffled his hair with a despairing gesture.

"I go now to cope with the cook. I never realized before what hard work housekeeping is."

Vivian laughed.

"Never mind," she said. "Think what a good husband you will make—one of the few men who will really appreciate domestic tribulations."

In spite of Mr. Andrews' complaints of the somewhat monotonous sameness of their meals, the food they enjoyed was quite passably appetizing.

Certainly Tony found nothing to complain about as he managed two and sometimes three helpings of nearly every dish.

In spite of his immense appetite, he could still chatter gaily as he ate, and it was he who tided over the somewhat stiff dinner-party that night.

Mr. Andrews had business at the monastery and could not return in time for the meal, so it was only the three of them who sat down in the small, candle-lit dining room.

Alec seemed rather quiet, and Vivian as usual, was constrained in his presence.

Only Tony talked on, making absurd jokes, finding conversation in nonsensical observations, and keeping Vivian laughing almost in spite of herself.

"Do you think Daddy is all right?" she asked Alec before they went up to bed.

"I hope so," he said gravely. "Everything depends on this. And tomorrow I want you and Tony to help me. As late as we dare in the morning, we must report that he is missing.

"I think it would look realistic if, in your anxiety, you rode over the plain as if in search of him. Bear to the east, of course, avoiding his real road."

"I cannot bear to think of him tonight, sleeping out in this bitter cold," Vivian said.

"Surdar has got the small tent with him," Alec reassured her. "They are going to throw it away before they are discovered by the search party.

"Honestly, you need not worry, Vivian, and your father himself seemed very confident when he left this morning. But I know how you feel. I wish I could help you."

"Thank you," Vivian said gently. "I am too old a campaigner really to fuss about him. It is only that this climate is so fantastic, and he is not a very young man."

Alec put out his hand and took hers.

"Good night," he said. "And try to sleep. I beg you not to worry."

There was so much kindness and understanding in his voice that Vivian had an insane desire to tell him that in spite of all he said and all the sense in his observations, she had a sudden premonition of danger.

It was so unlike her to be fearful, and yet the thought of her father battling against the bitter wind among the uncharted mountains filled her with dismay.

Then unexpectedly Alec kissed her hand.

She pulled it away from him. But the words she wanted to say died in her throat and she merely turned away and ran upstairs.

For a long time she walked up and down her room, and when finally she undressed and got into bed she could not sleep.

There seemed to be ever before her eyes the two figures,

struggling up the impassable paths and being lost in a strange, cruel darkness.

At last she got up, wrapping her dressing-gown around her, and, shivering a little with the cold, she lit a candle and crept down to the sitting room in search of a book.

The door was slightly ajar, and through it a kink of light streamed into the darkened passage.

Very cautiously, moving silently over the felt covering on the floor she looked in.

Alec was seated with his back to her at the writing desk. He was not writing or reading, but was leaning back in the chair, his head raised as if in thought.

Gently she moved away from the door and crept back to her bedroom. So Alec could not sleep either; he also kept vigil while the fate of his plans hung in the balance.

Alone in the darkness, Vivian prayed for her father and for his safety, and she knew, in spite of all they had said to her, that the odds were against his success.

* * * *

"I should take a coat with you."

Alec called from the doorway just as Vivian and Tony mounted their ponies ready for their long-planned ride in the pretended search for the Professor.

"Do you think we shall want them?" Tony asked.

Indeed it seemed unlikely for a brilliant sun made dark glasses and shady hats a necessity.

Alec walked slowly across the stone-paved courtyard before he replied, and, standing beside Vivian's mount, he spoke low so that his voice would not carry.

"I should make your ride a pretty long one," he said. "Don't forget that you are supposed to be consumed with anxiety as to your father's safety."

"There is not much supposition about that," Vivian said sharply.

"And also remember," Alec went on, taking no notice of her interruption, "that you must be looking around you just in hopes that you may sight him. Act your part, even if it appears to you that there is no one in sight. One never knows in this part of the world."

A moment later Tony, who had hurried indoors at Alec's suggestion that they should take coats, returned with them over his arm.

Made of heavy, undyed sheepskin, they were of local manufacture and were worn by all Tibetan travellers.

With the wool outside, and thickly lined, they were about the only possible garment which could withstand, to some extent, the biting afternoon winds.

Vivian threw hers across the front of her saddle and Alec tucked it into place.

"You may not get back before the wind rises," he said, "and I don't want you ill."

He spoke almost tenderly, but Vivian chose to misunderstand him.

"I should be an additional trouble, shouldn't I?" she said.

Then, without waiting for his reply, she flicked her horse lightly with her riding-whip and they moved off with a clatter of hooves towards the gateway of the courtyard.

"Good-bye, Alec," Tony called loudly. "We will come back with good news and the Doctor."

"The best of luck in your search," Alec replied loudly, also play-acting for whatever eavesdroppers there might be in the vicinity.

Vivian and Tony rode slowly and soberly towards the plain.

On their way, passing through the narrow streets of the town, Tony greeted friends and acquaintances, repeatedly explaining where they were going and their confident hope of finding the Doctor.

His cheery voice drew hordes of dark greasy women to the doorways, while whenever they stopped crowds of ragged urchins and eager sightseers surrounded the horses.

Sometimes they even ventured a question or two and Tony answered in halting Tibetan dialect.

"Already they know," he said to Vivian, "that your father is lost. News spreads like wildfire in this place. If you tell one official it is just the same as broadcasting anything in England!"

"Surely it was rather stupid of Alec," Vivian replied, "to let the cat out of the bag so soon?"

"Oh, he could not help himself," Tony replied. "Everything we do is reported by the servants. Half of them are spies, I am quite certain of that, and I should not be surprised if one or two of them can speak quite reasonable English."

"Nonsense," Vivian replied scornfully. "You are just frightening yourself about them. A more uneducated lot I have seldom seen."

"Well, anyway, that is Alec's theory," Tony said lightly. "And you notice how careful he always is at meals and at other times if there is the slightest chance of an eavesdropper. By the way, don't you like Alec?"

Taken by surprise at his question, Vivian did not answer for a moment or two, and then slowly, as if she were deeply considering, her answer seemed to be drawn from her almost again her will.

"I don't know," she said; "I honestly don't. I think, perhaps, to be truthful, I hate him."

"Hate Alec?" Tony ejaculated. "But it's impossible. Why, I think he is the best fellow in the world."

"Perhaps you don't know as much about him as I do," Vivian said.

"I think I do," Tony answered. "I have known him about three or four years now. I have seen him in bad times and good, and he is the most wonderful chap to those who work with him or under him."

He paused.

"Perhaps he is rather a man's man," he went on. "I don't think women are much in his line, but I've got the idea that he rather idealizes them."

"I certainly have not received that impression," Vivian said cynically.

"And do you know," Tony said, "I would like you two to be pals more than anything else in the world. Alec is the best man friend I have ever had and you . . ."

"And me?" Vivian questioned mischievously, smiling at him from under the shadow of her wide felt hat.

Tony flushed as he sought for words.

"Oh, I can't tell you now," he said hastily. "I will race you to those stones in the distance."

Laughing at his shyness Vivian accepted his challenge and a moment later they were riding neck to neck, spurring their steeds over the rough pebbled ground.

An hour or so later they were wandering in what seemed to Vivian a wilderness several miles from the town.

There was no sign of human habitation of any sort, only the monotonous barren and uneven ground stretching for mile after miles toward the mountains.

It was extraordinary how completely desolate one felt in such a world, where pasturage was a thing unknown and where one could ride for hours without meeting a living creature of any sort.

There were no birds in the sky, no rabbits or other small animals to scamper across one's path or detract from the utter loneliness.

The foxes and the wolves kept near the mountain sides, and even the Dro-pass or nomad herdsmen roamed the country on the higher plateaus where there was more and better pasturage to be found for their cattle.

The heat was almost overpowering at midday when Vivian and Tony, without dismounting, ate the sandwiches which they had brought with them and drank gratefully the barley water from their flasks.

"Do you think we have gone nearly far enough?" she asked a little later, wiping the beads of sweat from her forehead.

"Alec said we were to make a thorough job of it," Tony answered. "We had better go on a few more miles."

They trotted leisurely along, chatting as they did so.

They were just discussing their return when suddenly to the north of them a horseman appeared.

Vivian watched him idly for some moments while she was still chatting and then noticed that he was waving his arms in a strange manner.

"Do you think that man is signalling to us?" she asked Tony.

"Which man?" he questioned.

But before he could answer her question several other horsemen appeared behind the first. They joined him on the ridge.

"I wonder who they are?" Tony said anxiously. "They don't look much like travellers."

"Do you think they are robbers?" Vivian asked, remembering the horsemen she and her father had encountered in the Red Gorge.

"I hope to Heaven they are not," Tony said. "Look here, turn your horse around and let's return."

Vivian did as she was told and then perceived that on the southwest another band of horsemen were making their way leisurely toward them.

"I don't like this at all," Tony muttered.

Vivian did not reply, but her heart was beating quickly. It was quite obvious that the strange horsemen were converging on them from both directions.

Instinctively both she and Tony urged their horses into a gallop but a moment later a shot from the right-hand band rang out.

"What shall we do?" Vivian gasped, not slackening her pace.

"Keep low in your saddle," Tony shouted in reply.

Then before she could speak or even think a fusillade of shots greeted them.

The horsemen were getting nearer and the next moment Vivian felt her horse stop dead. She had a wild moment of fear, and she gave a shiver as she was flung over his head and crashed on to the ground.

A minute later, dazed and conscious of a throbbing pain in her head, she looked around her.

Her horse lay where it had been shot and from a gaping wound in its side poured a stream of blood. The strange horsemen had reined up in almost a circle around her.

As she raised herself to a sitting position she saw their faces, dark, fierce, and terrifying under broad-brimmed red hats strapped under their chins by wide leather bands.

The mist before her eyes gradually cleared. Her hat had fallen off as she fell, and with a trembling hand she pushed back the tumbled hair from her forehead.

She looked wildly for Tony. His horse was standing beside her fallen one. Already one of the strangers had dismounted and was holding it by the bridle.

Sagging in the saddle, his head down, his hands limp and lifeless, was Tony. With an effort Vivian dragged herself to her feet.

"Tony!" she cried. "Tony!" But she was prevented from going to him.

Her wrists were seized and bound behind her and even as she cried out in fear and misery they lifted Tony from the saddle.

She had a glimpse of his face, which terrified her, white and strange with closed eyes, and then before she could struggle she was picked up bodily and placed behind one of the strange horsemen on a wooden saddle.

A rope was tied around her waist and that of the man in front of her and then in a few seconds they were off, moving slowly but relentlessly in the direction of the mountains.

It seemed to Vivian, still dazed and shaken by her fall, that this must be some terrifying nightmare. She could not believe it was true.

Only the discomfort of the wooden saddle on which she was sitting, the pain of her fettered wrists, and the wide shoulders of her captor assured her that this was no dream.

With difficulty she managed to turn her head and glance behind her and saw that one of the other horsemen was carrying Tony across the front of his saddle.

Even in her deep anxiety for him it was still reassuring to know that he was being brought with her, dead or alive, to their unknown destination, wherever that might be.

There were over twenty horsemen in their little cavalcade, and she was thankful that they travelled quite slowly, due, she supposed, to the difficulty of hurrying with her and Tony as prisoners.

Even so, after a few miles she was in such an agony of discomfort that try as she would she could not prevent the tears from trickling down her face.

The Tibetans spoke very little among themselves, and Vivian realized that they were comparatively well-to-do.

Their harness was ornamented and studded with silver and precious stones, and their clothes, while dirty and smelly, were nevertheless of good material and in excellent repair.

The rifles slung round their shoulders were the most up-to-date she had seen.

The man behind whom she was riding carried his for some time in front of him and then he twisted it behind his shoulders so that it added agonizingly to her discomfort.

As she tried to move it into a less painful position she saw a name engraved on the butt, and after a moment of reading it almost automatically she realized that the writing was not in Tibetan.

With the jolting of the horse's movements it took her a moment or two to decipher it.

Then she knew that the rifle at which she was looking was of Russian pattern and manufacture.

Such knowledge increased her sense of fear, and almost at once she recalled the monk whom she had insulted in the street a week ago.

Alec had been nervous then of the consequences of her act. Were these, then, no ordinary robbers, but something more dangerous and even more to be feared?

A sudden panic overcame her. Her anxiety as to Tony's well-being had previously kept her from visualizing what might be her own fate, but now fear for her own immediate future made her tremble and she found her lips murmuring in prayer.

Supposing Tony were dead? Supposing they knew she was a woman? Supposing it was not ransom but revenge they were after?

At that moment Vivian would have welcomed unconsciousness. It seemed to her that her mental agony was a thousand times worse than her physical pain.

Feverishly she tried to calculate how long it would be before Alec realized that something unforeseen had occurred.

Ordinarily they would have been home at four o'clock. At five, perhaps, he would become really anxious, but by that time they would be—where?

Vivian sank forward, letting her head rest in numbed misery against her captor's back.

A little while later the cavalcade paused for a moment, but it was only so that the men could don their sheepskin coats against the wind which was beginning its stormy evening passage across the plain.

For a few moments Vivian's arms were free so that she might put on her own coat. But before the circulation could flow back into them they were secured again tighter than ever, and once more the men remounted and were off.

The cold got worse and more intense until Vivian became paralyzed and stupefied both in brain and body.

She was, indeed, almost unconscious two hours later when they ascended a steep hill, at the summit of which was a great stone Dzong.

She did not even notice as they passed through a huge gateway into a large, dirty courtyard.

Here, for the first time, the horsemen loosened their tongues. They shouted and called and from the doorways came running men, attendants and servants.

117

Rough hands pulled Vivian off the saddle and would have stood her on the ground had she not tottered and fallen.

She was then lifted bodily and carried up a rickety creaking stairway on to the veranda which led on to the first floor of the house.

She was just conscious of being carried through several huge, firelit rooms, before they passed through a small doorway. She was flung brutally onto the floor and the door slammed behind her captors.

For a long time she lay still, too numbed with cold and misery to move, one arm doubled under her, her eyes closed and her cheek resting against the rough felt substance which served for floor covering.

Then gradually the blood began to tingle in her wrists, and fingers, causing her greater and more acute pain than she had felt before.

Hours later, it seemed to her, there was the sound of bolts and bars being moved outside, the door was opened, and a man entered.

She cringed away from him almost instinctively, but he thrust towards her a large wooden bowl which he carried in his hand.

As she made no effort to take it he banged it down on the floor at her feet and then left as swiftly as he had come.

There was a faint light in the room from an open aperture or window which looked into the big room beyond.

From there also came what heat there was, from a fire which Vivian found later was lit for the comfort of the upper servants and more important horsemen.

While from the room beyond again came the sound of drunken and noisy revelry.

At last she put out her hands towards the wooden bowl and found that it contained tea. She was not so much hungry as cold, and the burning liquid which she sipped slowly brought her some degree of comfort.

The tea was quite unlike the pleasant quality she had tasted at the Chumbi Monastery. It was of a very coarse kind and so much else had been added that it was a very thick soup.

However, she was grateful for anything which would warm her, and after a time she did in fact feel better.

The talking and noise of merrymakers continued far

into the night, but Vivian, worn out and exhausted, at last slept fitfully, stretched out on the hard floor and covered by her sheepskin coat.

In fact she was asleep when she was startled into terrified wakefulness by the door of her prison being roughly thrown open and the entry of two of her captors of the day before.

They brought her another bowl of tea and a kind of dough ball made of barley grains.

She tried to eat it while they watched, but found it impossible, and finally drank a little of the tea, and still holding her breakfast in her hand, was hurried out into the courtyard.

Her lack of appetite was to stand her in good stead, for this time instead of binding her wrists behind her they left her hands free so that she could continue to eat.

But she was roped around the waist as on the day before, and her still sore limbs felt the hard contact of the wooden saddle and knew that her ride today was going to cause her even more agony than it had the previous afternoon.

It was as yet barely dawn and she strained her eyes among the horses being saddled and the men arriving, grumbling and sullen, still buttoning on their clothes and adjusting their rifles, for a sight of Tony.

Every moment that she waited she grew more desperately afraid that he might have died in the night and that they would leave him behind.

Then at last her heart gave a leap as from one of the ground-floor rooms two men appeared bearing him in their arms.

She could do no more than catch a glimpse of him, and she did not know whether he was conscious or unconscious.

With a sharp command, the gateway of the courtyard was flung open and the horsemen cantered slowly out into the pale grey morning.

CHAPTER TEN

"Oh God, let me die," Vivian sobbed.

She made no pretense at courage now but sagged forward crying audibly in her misery.

Her limbs were chafed until they were bleeding sores, and every step the horse took seemed to cause a fiery pain to shoot all over her.

All day they had ridden, not stopping for food, for the Tibetans seldom eat except in the morning and the evening.

The sun blazed down until the heat was almost unbearable.

But now the wind had risen again, and she prayed only that she might find warmth and rest.

They had travelled comparatively slowly, and yet as they had not stopped since dawn Vivian knew that they must be many miles from where they had spent the previous night.

Of Tony she had seen nothing. Two men took it in turns to share his burden on the front of their saddles, but they kept at the rear of the cavalcade while Vivian's captor remained in front.

They clambered up steep, nearly perpendicular paths, they passed through narrow gorges, they rode by lakesides.

Nowhere did it seem to Vivian was there any circumscribed track which would give anyone following or searching for them the slightest clue as to the direction they had taken.

Hope, which had kept her courage up during the day, at last succumbed to her pain, and gradually her nerves gave way under the strain until she just sobbed without attempting to control her misery.

It was quite late in the afternoon when she was suddenly startled by all the horsemen giving a great shout, crying in high, fierce voices which echoed out in the distance.

She raised her head and through her tears she saw in front of them a great hill on the steep sides of which were built huge buildings rising tier upon tier to a great height.

Most of the walls were painted red and colored with strips of other vivid colors while the temple roofs rose peaked and carved in Chinese style.

Even before the noise of conch shells blared forth like thunder from the walls, Vivian saw the red-robed lamas come running in their hundreds to the entrance gates, shouting in triumph. She knew that she and Tony were prisoners in the dreaded and notorious monastery of Kunwa-pa.

Vivian was taken some way into the heart of the monastery—which was large enough to house at least seven or eight thousand monks—before her captor dismounted.

Surrounded by a chattering, excited throng of lamas they dragged her through the stone doorway of a large building.

She was half carried down a long dark corridor and then thrust into a low-ceilinged, stuffy and dirty room, the only furniture in which was a mattress on the floor in one corner.

Her guards, however, did not leave her immediately, and a moment later there were more footsteps in the corridor and Tony was carried in.

None too gently he was put down on the mattress and then the men, with some coarse joke which made them all laugh, went out, closing and barring the door behind them.

Numbed and agonized though she was Vivian dragged herself over the floor to Tony's side. She gazed in horror at his white face, which seemed to be drained of all color.

His hands fell limp and lifeless on either side of him, and his legs were bent as he had been laid down.

"Tony!" she whispered, tears streaming down her cheeks. "Tony!"

She could see that his clothes were matted and stained with blood.

Suddenly the whole misery and hopelessness of her position made her drop her head against him and cry with abandonment and agony she had never known before.

The fierceness and heart-rending bitterness of her tears seemed to relieve her in some way, and a little while later, composed and more controlled, she tried to make Tony more comfortable.

She realized that he had been shot in the back, but the coldness of his skin was not yet the chill of death, and when she felt for his heart she could feel it beating very faintly.

She covered him up with his own coat and with her own, moving about to try and keep warm without it.

In the corner of the cell she found a rough kind of fireplace, the floor and ceiling blackened from past fires. She looked around for some rubbish to burn and found a small stack of dried yak dung in one corner.

After that it took her but a few moments with the help of matches from Tony's pocket to get a fire going.

There seemed to be little or no outlet for the smoke, but the warmth was worth streaming eyes and a choking cough.

She stood stretching out her hands towards the blaze when a sudden sound made her turn. Tony's eyes fluttered half open and his mouth moved.

"Tony," she said gently, "Tony, what is it?"

He muttered incoherently and then his cracked lips murmured:

"Water."

He was alive! He was alive! Her joy and anxiety overcame her fear so that she raced to the wooden door, beating on it with her fists, screaming and crying aloud.

For some time the only sound was her own voice echoing and re-echoing, and then at last came the sound of footsteps.

Luckily she knew the word in Tibetan both for water and tea, and she cried them alternately until the footsteps receded again.

Hopefully she waited and the moments passed by like hours. Supposing they intended to take no notice! Supposing they did not care?

Tony seemed to have lapsed into unconsciousness, only the occasional nervous twitch of his lips showed that he was alive. Now and then she spoke to him, but he did not answer.

She piled the fire high and by its light watched his face.

122

Finally there came the noise of people approaching, and the door was flung open to admit two lamas, one carrying the ritualistic whip, the second with two bowls, one of tea and the other of barley flour.

The food was placed on the floor and then both men advanced to look at Tony. They spoke among themselves and Vivian, stepping forward, said in English:

"He must have a doctor. He is very ill."

She repeated "ill" in Tibetan and then the word "medicine" which she had also remembered.

The lamas took no notice of her, so she repeated it again and then the one with the whip flicked it at her, not savagely but more contemptuously as a man might brush a mongrel from his path.

Still talking between themselves they left the room barring the door behind them.

Vivian clenched her hands with rage. At that moment she could have shot them both with pleasure, and then she realized her helplessness.

"Alec," she whispered to herself, "Oh, Alec, come and find us."

Taking up the bowl of tea she carried it to Tony and tried to place some between his lips. A good deal was spilled, but a little of the liquid was swallowed, and then Vivian realized her own intense hunger.

She kneaded the barley flour as she had seen the Tibetans do by mixing it with a little of the tea and then ate it.

Finally she drank some of the tea, shuddering a little at the great blobs of fat which floated on the surface.

When she had finished she felt overcome by a great fatigue.

In the warmth of the fire her chafed limbs throbbed until her whole body seemed one great gnawing ache.

Her head dropped forward, and finally, half sitting, half lying, she fell asleep, while the fire crackled and sizzled on into the night.

Far, far away something disturbed her. It seemed to Vivian that her consciousness must fight itself back from a deep fog of oblivion. The voice continued to call and finally awakened her.

With a start she realized where she was, that her limbs were stiff and cramped with cold, and that Tony was calling her name. His voice was weak and low.

She struggled onto her knees beside him. In the flickering light of the dying fire she could see that his eyes were open now, his mouth moving ceaselessly murmuring her name.

"I am here, Tony," she said. "It is all right. It is I, Vivian."

For a moment he stared at her and then at last he murmured hoarsely:

"Where are we?"

"We are prisoners," she answered. "And I think we are in the Kun-wa-pa monastery. How do you feel?"

"I am frightened," he whispered. "Vivian, I cannot move."

Only his eyes in the strained white face were alive, and she realized for the first time how unnaturally still his body was. He lay exactly as he had been put down hours before.

"Are you in pain?" she asked, and felt a deep sense of relief when he answered:

"No, but I am thirsty."

With an effort she rose unsteadily to her feet, her cramped and sore limbs seeming hardly to respond to her will.

In the corner of the room were the wooden bowls which had been full earlier in the evening. Some of the tea still remained, but it was cold, congealed and greasy, unpleasant even to look at:

She came back despondently to Tony's side.

"There is nothing for you, my dear," she said. "What can I do? Even if they gave us water I think it would be madness to drink it here."

"Give me a cigarette," he begged.

She searched in the pocket of his coat until she found his cigarette-case and lit one for him, holding it between his lips and removing it now and again as he could not raise his own hands.

She was nervous even of doing this, for smoking she knew was considered very wrong in Tibet and tobacco was tabooed by the Tibetans in much the same way as opium is in Europe.

"I am so cold," Tony said after a little while.

His lifeless hand which lay on the mattress beside Vivian

was so terribly chilled that even her own warm hands could not bring any warmth into it.

She rose and piled up the fire with the remaining stock of fuel. She wondered if the lamas would give them any more, knowing that if they passed many nights without warmth they would not be alive one morning to tell the tale.

Tony spoke once or twice and then relapsed, his eyes closed, and Vivian watched over him until a faint grey light through the chinks of the wooden shutter told her that dawn had broken.

She rose and unbarred the heavy wooden doors which closed an aperture in the wall that served as a window and which was guarded with thick iron bars.

Outside she could look down on the lower roofs of the monastery but there was no thoroughfare and she could see no sign of human beings.

Beyond the straggling untidy village lay the yellow plain, barren and desolate in the early morning light and devoid of any sign of humanity.

Vivian's heart sank. It seemed that here, indeed, she was cut off from all hope of rescue. Beyond the plain lay the mountains they had traversed the day before; treacherous, uncharted, uncrossed by any save the Tibetans themselves.

What hope had she and Tony of being found, at any rate soon enough to save them from a lingering and painful death from privation and cold, if from nothing worse?

With a little despairing gesture she slammed the shutters too again, preferring the warm fetid stuffiness of her prison to the sharp tang of the wind blowing in from outside.

She smoothed the hair back from Tony's forehead, she wrapped the sheepskin coats more closely around him, but there was nothing else she could do.

Were she to move him, even if it were possible, for he was a very heavy weight, to search for the wound in his back, she could have done nothing for him without water or bandages of any sort.

She was utterly helpless and she could only pray hopelessly and despairingly that by some miracle help would come to them.

She kept thinking of Alec. Would he realize what had happened to them? And if he did how could he save them?

An hour later their prison door was kicked roughly open

and two men entered. To Vivian's surprise one carried a sackful of fuel, the other a large, dirty cauldron filled with tea.

This he hung on an inverted nail over the fire, and he threw at Vivian's feet a small black bag of animal skin, such as peasants and travellers use to carry tsampa or barley flour.

They opened the shutters and then, after glancing around the bare confines of the cell, left.

Vivian wondered at this attention, but she was grateful even for small mercies, and when the tea was heated she filled the bowl they had used the night before and managed to make Tony swallow some of the hot liquid.

She was startled a little later by hearing the sound of voices and the tramp of many feet outside in the passage.

The explanation was soon forthcoming for once more the door was opened and red-robed lamas of a higher order than had visited them hitherto came crowding into the room.

They, however, merely preceded another man who, Vivian realized at once, must be a lama, or perhaps an Abbot, of great importance.

He wore Chinese robes beautifully embroidered, on his head was a pointed red cap with turned-up ear flaps, and in one ear was a long pendant earring of coral silver which showed that by birth he was one of the aristocracy.

His attendants, huge, surly men, carried large whips of yak-skin and flicked them about insolently, even towards the more humble attendant monks.

The Abbot stared at Vivian and then drew near to Tony's mattress. Vivian watched him without speaking.

He was not a young man and it seemed to her that as well as ferocious cruelty in his face there were also lines of dissipation and evil living.

Tony was unconscious. His eyes were closed. One of the attendants prodded him in the side with his whip and then lashed him across the legs with the thong. Vivian started forward in anger.

"How dare you strike a sick man!" she cried. "Can't you see how desperately ill he is? Perhaps he is even dying."

Her words were unintelligible, but the tone of her voice and her anger could not be misunderstood.

She confronted the lamas with blazing eyes, her head

flung back, her hands clenched, very slim and defiant in her riding clothes, and they could not guess at the desperate fear in her heart.

They stared at her for a moment as if surprised at her interruption, and then addressing herself to the chief man she added:

"We are English. You have no right to bring us here and keep us prisoners. I demand that we be returned to Gyangtse."

Whether he understood her or not she had no idea, but she was past caring, a white heat of fury driving her to speak loudly and defiantly.

"I demand it," she said. "This is an outrage you have perpetrated."

The Abbot raised his hand reflectively to his shaven chin.

He looked her over with dark, searching eyes, and then he spoke in a low voice to one of the men at his side.

Without any warning the man stepped forward towards Vivian and before she could recoil or even move he seized the collar of her riding shirt with both his hands and tore it apart.

There was the sound of rending cloth and a smothered scream from Vivian as she stood before them half naked, revealing all too clearly that it was no young man defying the staring officials.

Desperately her hands caught the torn silk around her, covering her breasts from the evil eyes which humiliated and seared her very soul.

A faint smile seemed to flicker at the corner of the Abbot's lips and then he turned and led the way from the room.

The monks followed him, those in the rear staring back as they went, and it seemed to Vivian that their glances were not only curious but lecherous.

As the door closed behind them she rushed forward seeking a bolt or barrier on the inside with which she could bar them out, but there was none.

Her hands stretched out over the rough, unplaned surface of the door seeking some defense, some security. For a moment she stood as if crucified, and then with a little sob she sank despairingly on to the floor, her head resting on her bent arms.

Low voices outside made her jump to her feet again like some startled animal.

She shrank away, trying with trembling fingers to repair her torn shirt.

Then slowly, very slowly, the door opened again to admit the most terrifying apparition she had ever seen.

Dirty, greasy robes, which had once been red but had long since become so spattered with filth covered a man whose face was smeared with dirt and whose dark, uncut hair hung in long wisps to his shoulders.

Around his neck were rosaries made of carved human bones, and hanging from his waist were strange and weird objects, among them a skull and a female femur, which told Vivian that she was in the presence of a Tantrik sorcerer.

She had seen one or two on their journey to Gyangtse and had been amazed at the fear and reverence with which they were treated by the people.

She had heard a little from her father of their disgusting practices, of the way they treated corpses and their methods of preying on the superstitious people.

No one in Tibet would willingly cross the wishes of a sorcerer. They know only too well what would be the result of such defiance.

Their cattle would die; they themselves would suffer from strange, incurable sicknesses; thunderstorms would damage their meager crops, and all their friends would shun them as a man who has been cursed.

In some cases, the herbs prescribed by these Asiatic witch doctors proved efficacious, but most of their tricks were based on magic.

The terrifying sorcerer came a few feet into the room, and then began chanting a strange and vibrating mantram.

His voice rose and fell harshly, and the monks who had admitted him closed the door behind him so that he was alone with Vivian and the unconscious Tony.

She moved towards the mattress where Tony lay, feeling that he was some protection, helpless as he was, against her own fear of what might be about to happen.

The sorcerer continued to chant, moving slowly nearer and nearer the sick man.

His whole condition, his filthy appearance, and his

strange accoutrements, fascinated Vivian, so that she could not take her eyes from him as she stood watching his approach.

How could she stop him touching Tony, she wondered. How could she prevent this bestial creature from mauling the sick man?

All the tales she had been told of the superstitions, the orgies of devil worship, and the violation of decency by the Tantrik followers came back in wild, distorted fragments to her mind.

Nearer and nearer the sorcerer advanced, and then, ceasing to chant, he spread out his hands.

Almost involuntarily Vivian leapt to her feet to protect Tony. She would have shrieked, but her voice seemed to choke in her throat from sheer terror.

Then, in a whisper, the sorcerer said:

"It is all right. Don't be afraid."

For a moment Vivian thought she had gone mad. She stared at him, her mouth slightly open, her eyes dilated.

Only after what seemed an aeon of time did it sink fully into her awareness that he had spoken English.

"It is I," the sorcerer said, still speaking almost beneath his breath.

Then at last she knew and her heart leapt with an almost agonizing relief.

It was Alec! Alec in disguise. As Vivian realized it the reaction was too much.

She could not speak, only great tears welled into her eyes and flowed down her cheeks, her mouth trembling, her hands fluttering out towards him.

"Be careful!" he commanded sharply.

"Oh, Alec, Alec!" she whispered. "How did you know? How did you find us?"

"Never mind that now," he said swiftly. "There is no time to be lost. You have got to get out of here and get out quickly. I know what they are planning."

His mouth set in a sharp line as if even he felt the horror and terror of what might happen.

Then he bent over Tony, moving him gently but firmly, turning him over on his face until he could see the hideous and gaping wound where he had been shot in the back.

Without speaking, Vivian watched. The blood and condition of the wound made her feel faint, so that for a moment everything swam before her eyes, but biting her lips, she kept control of herself.

She knew that her courage would be required for worse things than this, and yet the pity of it made her want to cry out in protest.

Tenderly, but with sure fingers, Alec dressed the wound.

Already there was a deep discoloration around it, and Vivian knew, from her own meager knowledge of first aid, though she dared not admit it to herself, that such a condition must prove fatal without a surgeon.

When he had finished, and Tony was lying unconscious on his back, Alec slipped some pellets between his lips and then said to Vivian:

"I shall come again at dawn tomorrow. Be ready to come with me."

"But Tony. How can we leave Tony?" she asked urgently.

Very gently Alec passed his hand over the young man's forehead. Even beneath the dirt and stain on his face, Vivian could see the tenderness and compassion of his expression.

"Tony will not live through the night," Alec said, very quietly. "If he did, by some miracle, he would be paralyzed."

"It can't be true," Vivian said in sudden agony. "Tell me it isn't true. Oh, Alec!"

"Hush!" he said warningly.

As if to cover the emotion in her voice, which she had raised inadvertently, he started to chant again, and still chanting moved towards the door.

He knocked commandingly on its surface, and instantly it was opened from without, and not vouchsafing another glance in Vivian's direction, he passed out of her sight and again she was alone.

When he had gone she sat staring at the door, as if she could hardly believe his presence had been other than a dream or a delusion.

Could Alec really have appeared, have walked into the monastery in such a disguise that no one could possibly have known him?

Her heart was beating in thankfulness, and yet there were still tears in her eyes at what he had told her about Tony.

Dear Tony, lying there so white and still. Never again would he laugh and tease her, would they play their absurdly childish games, would he make love to her with boyish awkwardness.

It seemed so unfair, so cruel.

"I can't bear it, I can't bear it! It can't be true!" Vivian stormed within herself.

Yet she had seen the wound in his back, and she knew it must prove fatal.

The shot had penetrated the spine, and she knew Alec spoke the truth when he said that were Tony to live, which would only be possible if modern surgery could be procured, now and at once, he would be paralyzed.

"No," she told herself. "It is more merc'ful."

The pills Alec had given him had seemed to lull him into a still deeper unconsciousness and his breathing was slightly heavier.

"Thank God, he has suffered no pain," Vivian thought, as all through the long, hot hours of the day she watched Tony's white face.

She did not wonder, as yet, how Alec was going to aid her, she only knew that she trusted him implicitly when he promised to come for her, and she knew that he would not break his word.

In the afternoon the wind got up and soon she shuttered the window and stoked up the fire.

She made herself eat and drink, knowing that all her strength would be needed in the coming ordeal.

The black bag full of barley flour she kept prominently before her, feeling that it would be wise to take it with them in case of necessity.

As the hours passed, Tony seemed to be sinking, his breathing grew fainter and fainter, and when she felt his heart the beat was almost indiscernible.

Once he opened his eyes and looked at her, but when she spoke to him he did not answer, only a very faint smile touched his lips, then wearily he slept again.

Vivian had no watch and it seemed to her that never had twenty-four hours passed so slowly. Every minute seemed like an hour, and she found herself counting the seconds . . . sixty . . . one minute gone . . . another sixty . . . two minutes gone.

If only Alec would come. She felt that if he prolonged

his appearance he might find her almost demented with sheer anxiety. And then at last fear began to torment her.

Supposing he had been discovered? Supposing his disguise had been penetrated? He also might be languishing in prison, perhaps already being tortured.

Vivian knew that one of the favorite tortures of the Tibetans was to kill a yak, skin it, and sew a prisoner into the still warm skin, and then leave it in the blazing sun.

The heat would contract the outer covering so that slowly but surely the person imprisoned inside would be suffocated to death.

Other tortures, diabolical ones, came half remembered and unwanted to her mind, until sheer exhaustion forced her to lie down on the floor and rest her aching head on her arms.

Fitfully she dozed, waking at every slight sound, and the long, long night passed like a century. When finally the door was opened and she heard the low chanting of the sorcerer only caution prevented her from crying out with joy.

She got to her feet, and then the gladness on her face faded into a horrified stare as she saw in terror that this time Alec was accompanied by a red-robed lama.

He was also a sorcerer, but not such an uncouth, creature in appearance. He wore the traditional red hat of the monastery and he carried a trumpet made of a human shin bone and rosary of carved bones.

A small, almost insignificant man, he peered at Vivian by the light of the flickering butter lamp which he carried, and then at Tony.

"So Alec's plans have gone awry," Vivian thought with a sinking of her spirits.

This was the end, then, he could not help her. She turned away to hide the expression of her face, which she feared might reveal to the stranger that something was amiss.

Almost immediately, Alec broke into the chanting mantram with which his first visit had been preluded. His voice rose and fell as he approached the sick man.

Vivian stood aloof, watching him in an agony of unhappiness and misery so that she could only think over and over again—"Alec has failed."

Slowly he approached the mattress, and then, turning to his companion, beckoned him forward.

The monk came nearer, bending to have a better look at Tony, and even as he did so Alec raised the heavy bone which hung at his waist and brought it down with all his force on the back of the monk's head.

It was so surprising, so swift, that Vivian could hardly forbear to give a startled exclamation.

The monk fell like a log, and Vivian sprang forward to pick up the lamp which dropped from his hand.

"Quick," Alec commanded Vivian in a whisper. "Help me get his clothes off."

Startled and amazed, Vivian did as she was told, dragging the greasy red robes from the prostrate body and taking the human trumpet, the rosary, and the other paraphernalia from his neck and waist. With swift fingers Alec gagged and bound the man with rags torn from his own clothing.

"Your sheepskin coat," he said to Vivian.

She picked it up and helped Alec to wrap it around the seminaked body of the unconscious man.

Lifting him bodily in his arms, Alec staggered with his burden into a corner, and there arranged him in a recumbent position as if he were asleep.

Vivian stood watching, too dazed by the swiftness of events to question or even surmise what was to be the next move.

"Be quick," Alec said to her. "Put on his things."

"Put them on?" Vivian echoed, and then understood.

She shuddered a little as the greasy red robe, smelling abominably, touched her skin, and she hated the cap which fitted over her head and was pulled low on her eyebrows.

From his rags Alec produced a thick grease which he swiftly smeared over her face and neck, rubbing into it dirt and ashes from the fireplace and performing the same operation on both her hands.

Only when he had finished and she could feel a thick layer of dirt covering her face, did he speak again.

"Keep your head bent," he commanded, "and follow me. Whatever happens, don't look about you or seem surprised or afraid. This is our only chance and a thin one. It is up to you."

"And Tony?" Vivian whispered.

Only then did Alec turn towards the mattress and touch Tony's forehead and feel his heart.

Something in his silence and in the way he tried again and again to find a heartbeat told Vivian that quietly, and without a single farewell, Tony had died. She gave an inarticulate little sob.

Instantly Alec stood and turned to her.

"I know, my dearest," he said very tenderly. "But it is better so. He did not suffer in the slightest."

Vivian moved towards the mattress. She dropped on her knees for one moment, and then on an impulse she pressed her lips to Tony's forehead.

The chill of his skin brought home to her even more vividly that Tony had indeed left them.

"God keep you," she murmured brokenly.

Then, rising to her feet, she looked Alec straight in the eyes.

"I am ready," she said bravely.

CHAPTER ELEVEN

"I can't go any further," Vivian cried, her breath coming in sobbing gasps.

The sweat was pouring down her face, making streaks through the grease and dirt.

"You have to," said Alec sternly. "We must reach the mountains as quickly as possible."

"I can't! I can't!" she cried, dragging her legs in utter weariness, weighed down by the heavy folds of her disguise.

Alec reached out and took her arm, holding it above the elbow in a fierce, almost cruel, grip.

"Hurry," he said sternly.

Hating him she struggled on, too weary, too exhausted to protest, half blinded by the glaring sun, her mouth parched, her lips dry.

It was over three hours since they had left the monastery. They had walked out of the prison past the guards at the entrance and turned toward the lower gate.

Although it was early the lamas were already moving about, some carrying fuel, others hurrying towards the great courtyard.

Vivian's heart was beating almost suffocatingly. She felt that every man they encountered looked at her suspiciously.

But the sorcerer and his disciple created little interest.

A few lamas made a gesture of greeting or spoke to Alec as they passed, but otherwise their progress was uneventful until they reached the great wooden gate with its pagoda top which was the entrance to the monastery itself.

Here, in front of the guardian deities, were colossal fierce images with projecting teeth, holding in their hands human skulls and waving with one of their many arms the magic sword and the inverted triangles of the sacred circle.

Before them Alec made a deep obeisance and Vivian, terrified, stiffly followed his example.

Slowly the guards swung open the doors. Beyond lay the dirty village, the dusty plain, and freedom.

As they walked slowly through the gates Vivian expected every moment to hear shouts and yells or to receive a bullet in her back, but they passed without trouble through the refuse-strewn streets.

On and on they went, slowly and with dignity, until finally they stood on the edge of the plain itself, and then Alec started to move swiftly.

The sun rose and its fierce heat seemed almost overpowering, and yet Alec's pace never abated.

Cruelly, it seemed to Vivian, he forced her on with stern commanding words, ignoring her pleas for just five minutes' rest.

For a time she walked almost mechanically, her mind dazed and dizzy with thoughts and fears.

Then the aching weariness of her limbs and the exhaustion which seemed to be rapidly overpowering her made her cry out again and again.

Alec's fingers bit into her soft flesh and the pain, combined with her anger at his unkindness, seemed, in spite of herself, to spur her on to further efforts.

Occasionally she stumbled against the tufts of coarse grass and each time she felt as though, were she to fall, she could never rise again, whatever fate should befall her.

The tortures of the lamas, the evils of the black faith, even the horrors of flayed human skins and magic obscenities paled beside the misery she was enduring under the relentless burning sun.

She knew that Alec was right and that their only hope of escape when their crime was discovered was to have reached the hills where there was some chance of hiding from the pursuing bands of horsemen.

On the plains there was not enough cover to shelter a rabbit, let alone human fugitives. Fast as they had traveled it would not take a horse a quarter of the time to catch up with them.

While Vivian might imagine vaguely the punishment which would await them should they be recaptured, it was

Alec, who knew grimly whatever happened neither of them must be taken alive.

An hour passed and still they struggled forward until at last they reached the foot of the hills.

The ascent was not gradual for the mountainous formations of Tibet are the remains of volcanic eruption.

The mountains rise almost perpendicularly from the flattest of plains and descend just as abruptly.

Scrambling on the loose stone paths which had been formed by the passage of melting snows or by the natural formation of the rocks themselves Vivian and Alec climbed higher and higher.

At times it seemed to Vivian that her heart would burst. Every breath was painful, every step required greater and greater effort.

Only her fear of Alec drove her on.

"I shall die," she sobbed once, tears choking her voice. "Go on and let me stay. I would risk anything rather than this."

"Get up," he commanded abruptly. "This is no time for weakness."

Again her anger and her hatred of him made her do what seemed impossible.

"I hate you," she told him once, as she slipped and fell, cutting her knees against a sharp grey stone.

"I am concerned with your safety, not your feelings," he said curtly. "I had no idea you were so weak."

"Weak," she murmured between her teeth. "Could anyone stand this torture without being broken by it?"

"Oh, a good many people," he said lightly.

Flicked by the disdain in his voice she crawled on and upwards. Finally, when all before her eyes was black and dizzy, when the blood pumping in her temples sounded like a great gong, she heard Alec say in an almost unbelievably kind voice:

"Now you can rest."

She dropped like a stone just where she was, lying full out, the sweat pouring over her body, trickling even from her fingertips.

Only after a long time of what seemed to Vivian exquisite oblivion did she open her eyes and realize where she was.

Under the shadow of a great rock they perched high on

the mountainside, while the plain lay hundreds of feet below them.

As she looked up, feeling almost divorced from her body which seemed to have slipped away from her on a tide of fatigue, she saw Alec was peering anxiously to where half-a-day's journey away lay the monastery of Kun-wa-pa.

She watched him for a moment and then he must have known of her scrutiny for without turning his head in her direction he said:

"Are you feeling better?"

"I think I am just alive."

"Then we must go on."

"Go on!" Vivian cried in dismay.

She was aware that it was inevitable even while she shrank from the thought of torturing her body still further.

"Aren't we safe?" she asked.

Alec turned and then looked at her almost incredulously.

"Safe?" he said. "My dear girl, you will never be safe in this country again. The sooner we get out of it the better."

He rose to his feet.

"Come on," he said. "There is no time to be lost."

The afternoon wind swept and battered them, penetrating their fluttering clothes and drying their skins after the heat of the day, until their limbs and their faces felt agonizingly sore.

Alec never faltered. He seemed instinctively to know the right direction and the right path to choose, striking out across an unfrequented part of the hills.

Nightfall came swiftly, but just before darkness fell Alec swerved aside from their course and clambering about fifty feet upwards discovered a small cave in the side of the rock.

Vivian had long since given up speaking or even protesting. She had walked, mile after mile, conscious only of numbed fingers, of a body too cold to shiver, of blistered heels and a paralyzing tiredness which was too intense to be sensed.

She felt that nothing worse could happen to her, that death itself would be preferable.

She knew that were she to stop Alec would spur her on, and in her misery she was too afraid of his scorn and sarcasm to do anything but follow him about twenty paces behind as he walked relentlessly into the wind.

The cave was a small one and smelt strongly of fox but it was unoccupied by any form of life at the moment.

Vivian lay on the floor of it with closed eyes while Alec placed together a few pieces of fuel he had gathered on the route during the last hour or so and coaxed them to light.

From his tattered and dirty garments he pulled out the black pot which all Tibetan travellers carry as their only cooking utensil.

He had to scramble several hundreds of feet away from the cave in the growing dark to discover a drift of snow, on the northern side of a peak, which had remained un-melted in spite of the burning sun.

Half ice and half snow, he filled the pit, threw into it a block of tea and added salt and a little butter in the true Tibetan fashion.

When it was ready he woke Vivian, who had already passed into an exhausted slumber, and insisted on her filling the bowl which was concealed in her borrowed robes and made her drink.

Amazingly the warmth and nourishment revived her as she felt the fiery liquid coursing down her throat.

She made an effort to swallow some of the barley flour dipped into it and rolled into a dumpling.

"There was no need for us to have butter and salt in the tea," she said. "There is no one to see us here."

"It is more nourishing than you realize," Alec said, "also the tea is of such poor quality that I do not think it would be more appetizing without the other ingredients. Travel-ing sorcerers cannot afford better so it is no use complain-ing."

"After this I shall never complain about anything again," Vivian replied.

"Well, go to sleep as quickly as you can," he com-manded. "The moment the dawn breaks we must start off again."

It was not difficult for her to obey him and she slept on the hard dirty floor of the cave better than she had ever done in any soft, luxurious bed.

Yet it seemed to her that she had hardly closed her eyes before Alec was shaking her into wakefulness, his voice dragging her back to awareness of their miserable sur-roundings and the aching misery of her own body.

She felt too tired to speak. Dawn had only just broken, pale and grey, and it cast a faintly depressing light into their small cave.

It was bitterly cold in spite of the fire which Alec had kept burning all night, and Vivian accepted gratefully the bowl of boiling tea which he held out to her.

"I must repair your disguise," Alec said as she swallowed her unappetizing breakfast.

For the first time since they had started on their desperate journey Vivian thought of her appearance and realized how ghastly she must look—but this was no time for vanity.

Alex rubbed his fingers on the blackened bottom of the pot in which he had cooked their tea and smeared the greasy soot on her face, pulling her red cap low over her forehead and treating her hands to another coat of blacking.

For the first time Vivian laughed.

"We must look awfully funny," she said, and Alec smiled back at her in return.

"We have got a long way to go," he said.

With something like dismay Vivian realized how terribly exhausted she was already.

Without another word Alec started to stamp out the fire, packing the cooking utensils into the greasy yakskin bag, and then they slithered down the steep incline from their cave on to the winding, stony way which lay below.

For the first few hours Vivian tried to take an interest in the country through which they were passing, looking for the distant glimmer which told her they were approaching one of the numerous lakes.

She tried to remember that every footstep was bringing her nearer home and nearer security, and then it was as if she because unconscious of everything except the knowledge that she must go on and on.

Fear spurred her on—fear of Alec; until he seemed to her like some monster driving her forward, and once she imagined him as a great powerful eagle carrying her away as if she were some defenseless, quivering animal.

"That is what he is," she thought.

The title seemed curiously appropriate to the hard, almost steely glitter in his eyes, the strong line of his mouth and chin, the square shoulders, and the indomitable will which kept her going even when it seemed a physical impossibility.

All through the long hours of blazing sunshine they moved steadily forward, keeping as far as possible from any familiar ground.

They did not speak as they trudged on, and Vivian knew that it was useless to voice her miseries.

Nothing worse than this could happen to her, she thought more than once.

"Can't we rest?" she gasped.

But Alec shook his head and kept steadily on, walking in front of her while she, as was correct for the sorcerer's disciple, trailed along a few feet behind him.

They skirted the herds of yaks which they saw, afraid that the dro-pas might give information were they questioned later by pursuing horsemen.

They made a wide detour of the one small village with a few miserable houses which nestled at the foot of a small hill on which was built the inevitable stone castle.

All too soon the bitter wind started to blow, developing in a few moments into a tearing, biting gale, and then at last Vivian did collapse.

She tried to battle her way forward against the wind but finally, with a pitiful cry, she dropped in a crumpled heap on the ground and hid her face in the tattered red sleeves of her robes.

"I can't go on, I can't," she sobbed. "It is no use."

On the ground she was, for the moment, out of the force of the wind and she lay cowering there expecting to hear Alec's voice raised in command and knowing that whatever he said now it would be impossible to obey him.

She felt so numbed with cold and pain that she was not afraid any more. She knew that her courage and her will had deserted her and that she was utterly beaten.

To her surprise Alec did not speak and then she felt his hands touch her shoulders.

She quivered in sudden fear, of what she did not know, and then he gathered her up in his strong arms, lifting her as if she were a baby, and carrying her, with her face high against his chest.

"Don't, Alec," she protested weakly. "Please...don't..."

He took no notice and she was too exhausted to speak again.

They went on for perhaps fifty yards, and then Alec found shelter behind a broken wall of stone. There he put her down and she lay back with closed eyes grateful that for the moment she could not feel the force of the gale.

"I am going to leave you here," Alec said.

With a little cry of horror she opened her eyes and stretched out her hands instinctively towards him.

"Leave me," she said. "You can't mean that."

He knelt down beside her, taking her hands tenderly and putting them into her long sleeves, wrapping the hem of her robe around her legs tightly.

"Only for a little while," he said soothingly. "I am going back to the village we passed a little while ago. If it is possible I shall buy or hire horses. I daren't light a fire in case it attracts attention.

"Just sit here and if by chance someone comes near you intone, as you have heard me do, the sacred Tibetan words. No one will interrupt you until you have finished and you must go on until I return."

Vivian was so tired she could hardly understand what he was saying to her but she tried to force herself to attend.

Only as he rose to his feet did she say in a terrified whisper:

"Oh, Alec, is it dangerous? For you, I mean," she added.

"Don't you worry," he said cheerfully. "I will come back to you. Good-bye, my darling."

Without another word he turned and strode away and after a moment she could see him no more.

She lay completely still, feeling that at any moment her mind would escape her and she would sink into a deep, unconscious oblivion.

But those last words of Alec's kept her awake, for they rang in her ears; the tone of his voice as he had called her "my darling," and she remembered the tender way his hands had touched her.

"Does he really love me?" she asked herself.

Somehow it seemed absurd in this atmosphere of fear and cold to be thinking of love.

Yet Alec had rescued her, had taken her away from the monastery, had brought her so far in safety.

142

And she knew almost intuitively, however great her fears that somehow, in some indomitable manner he would get her back to Gyangtse.

She sank lower against the wall and her head dropped on her chest, wave after wave of exhaustion sweeping over her; yet she did not lose consciousness.

Once above the roar of the wind she thought she heard voices and every nerve in her body was startled into a terrified alertness.

She was alone. If the pursuing monks should find her now she would receive no mercy at their hands. Even travellers were almost as greatly to be feared, for they loathed all foreigners.

She was outside the protectorate of Gyangtse, and would, if she were allowed to live at all, be treated with barbaric cruelty if her disguise were penetrated.

She found herself praying for Alec's return. It was getting darker every minute, the afternoon was drawing to a close.

Even the bitter cold and her own aches and pains were forgotten in her fears, and she prayed, clenching her hands together until the nails bit into the flesh.

At last when it seemed that her terror must drive her mad she heard the clatter of horses' hooves approaching. They came nearer and nearer, but she dared not move in case it was not Alec.

Then at last, above the noise of the wind, she could hear someone whistling and her heart leapt as she knew it was indeed Alec and he was signaling to allay her fears.

With a little cry she staggered to her feet and stood staring into the darkness awaiting him, listening with a faint smile on her lips to the tune of "Keep the home fires burning."

"Thank you . . . God . . . thank you," she said in her heart, "for Alec."

*　*　*　*

"I thought you were never going to wake up again," Mr. Andrews said as he entered Vivian's bedroom.

"I can't believe this is true," Vivian answered from the bed.

"Do you know you have slept for twenty-four hours?" Mr. Andrews asked.

He drew up a chair beside the bed and sat down.

"I am only surprised that it was not twenty-four days," Vivian replied. "I can hardly remember getting back, I was so utterly exhausted, but I remember that ride."

She sighed.

"It seemed interminable, as if the night would never end; and when at last as the dawn broke we saw Gyangtse lying in the plain below us I thought it was a mirage. Where is Alec? Is he all right?"

"He is all right in himself," Mr. Andrews answered. "But . . ."

"Well, what is it now?" Vivian said. "Are we going to be besieged or something?"

"It isn't that," Mr. Andrews replied.

"Well, what is it?" Vivian asked soberly.

"It is your father," Mr. Andrews said gently. "He has not returned."

Vivian sat up in bed and stared at him.

"He left last Tuesday," she said, "and he should have met the search party on Saturday . . . Now it is Tuesday again. What can have happened?"

"That is just what we are worrying about," Mr. Andrews said. "The search party were at the appointed place as had been arranged, but he did not turn up."

"Does Alec think he has lost his way?" Vivian asked.

"Of course that is what he thinks," Mr. Andrews said severely. "Alec won't be back until dinnertime and we will all have to wait for news until then. You are to rest and, if possible, sleep. Those are my orders as your medical adviser in the absence of the Doctor."

"Are you quite certain there is nothing I can do?" Vivian asked.

"Absolutely nothing," he said, "and Alec's last instructions were that you were not to leave the Block House."

"Mr. Andrews," Vivian said, clenching her hands together, "you don't think anything really awful can have happened to Daddy, do you?"

"Nothing worse than being lost in the cold of the mountains," he answered firmly; "and they have got plenty of food with them and a tent. Honestly, Vivian, I don't think you need worry. Alec is certain to bring us some news tonight!"

He rose to his feet and walked towards the door.

"I will send you up a large lunch," he said smiling. "I expect you can manage it."

"I could eat a whole ox," Vivian said, "and then ask for more."

But when the door closed behind him the smile faded from her face, and was replaced by a worried frown.

Why hadn't her father returned? She had been too exhausted yesterday morning to realize that he was overdue.

As they rode into the courtyard of the Block House she was holding on to her horse's saddle, keeping herself awake by an almost superhuman effort of will.

For several hours she had been quite incapable of guiding her animal, and Alec had led her horse as though she were a child.

She had been carried upstairs to her bedroom and she had just been capable of sinking into the warm bath which had been prepared for her.

When she was in bed Mr. Andrews had brought her a long sleeping draught, and under its influence she had sunk away into a dreamless, healthy sleep.

She was stiff and sore, but her brain felt clear and refreshed, and apart from weakness she was none the worse for her adventure.

Only her skin, cracked from the burning heat of the days and the bitter cold of the night wind, showed evidence of what she had been through.

The whole episode seemed like some hideous dream, but now that she was back she knew that every moment in this house there would be one ghost which would haunt her incessantly.

Even now she found herself listening, as it were, for the sound of Tony's voice, the loud cheerful tones which had echoed through every room.

Vivian dreaded going downstairs. The dining room would bring back vivid memories of him, and so would the sitting room where they had laughed and played together.

"I shall have to write to his mother," Vivian said to herself.

Yet how could she possibly put in writing her regret at what had occurred, how could she explain to that woman sorrowing in England the hopeless tragedy of a young life wasted for no particular reason.

Lying in bed, Vivian felt a yearning to escape, to get away.

She had welcomed the idea of coming to Tibet because of the opportunity it had given her to leave England, but now she would give anything to be back in a country where she knew there was peace and security and no fear of violence or sudden death.

She remembered her presentiment the night her father left and it seemed to her now that it had been justified.

Tony dead—her father missing—she put up her hands and covered her face, but not to hide her tears. The whole thing seemed past the weak futility of weeping.

How exceedingly petty her unhappiness about Jimmy seemed now.

Love and Monte Carlo; England with its green fields; Jimmy marrying a rich wife; how far away they all were now.

All day Vivian waited for news of Alec's return. She slept a little and ate, finding that food revived her energy, so that by the evening she was glad to get up and dress.

Every muscle in her body was stiff and there were open sores on her legs which had to be dressed and bandaged, but otherwise she was amazed at the elasticity of her strength.

She dressed herself in a soft dinner gown of dark red lace. It had been an easy garment to pack and was one of the few attractive things among her very small supply of clothes.

When she had finished dressing she could not help a swift glance of satisfaction. Alec would see her looking herself.

He had however not yet returned and when finally dinner was ready, Mr. Andrews and Vivian sat down alone in the strangely quiet dining room.

Their conversation was disjointed and almost mono-syllabic.

Neither disguised the fact that they were listening every moment for the sound of horses' hooves on the courtyard outside.

"What can be keeping him?" Vivian said at last, her voice raw and sharp with anxiety.

But as she spoke they heard the sentry's challenge, the noise of the great wooden gate being drawn back, and the clatter of hooves on the cobbled yard.

Both Vivian and Mr. Andrews rose instinctively to their feet and stood looking toward the door until a moment later it was flung open and Alec entered.

Without waiting for him to speak, after one look at his face Vivian knew that he bore bad news. She moved across to him, put out her hand and took his.

He was very pale, his hair tousled, his clothes stained and dusty as though he had ridden hard and furiously. His fingers closed over hers, holding it in a taut hard grip.

It was Mr. Andrews who spoke first.

"What news, Alec?" he said.

But when Alec answered it was to Vivian he spoke and his voice was low and tense.

"Your father," he said, "is a prisoner."

Vivian gave a little choking groan. For a moment the room seemed to spin round her and only the grip of Alec's hand kept her from falling.

With an effort she put out her other hand and steadied herself against the table.

"My God!" Mr. Andrews ejaculated. "How do you know?"

Without speaking Alec guided Vivian back to her chair. She sat down, her hands gripping the wooden arms, her eyes, dark and tragic, fixed on his face.

Only when she was seated did Alec turn to Mr. Andrews.

"Give me a drink," he said.

He sat down at the table as if utterly exhausted. Mr. Andrews gave him a whisky-and-soda and he drank it off in one gulp.

"We found Surdar this afternoon," he said abruptly, his strong voice grave and harsh with emotion. "He had been mortally wounded and was dying when I got to him. He just managed to tell me what had happened, then he died in my arms."

Vivian sat as if turned to stone. Mr. Andrews made an ejaculation. They waited for Alec to go on.

"It was the Russian syndicate," he continued. "Surdar was quite sure of their nationality. They had two Tibetan guides with them but the men in charge were Russians.

147

They came upon the Professor and Surdar quite unexpectedly.

"The Professor started to explain that they were lost, the tale we had prepared, of course, but they gave him no time. One of the men addressed him in English, according to Surdar, and then searching him they found his rough notes and glasses.

"At the point of a revolver they made him get on one of their horses and then rode off towards the west.

"Only before they went, at the Russians' command, one of the Tibetan guards turned round and shot Surdar through the chest."

"The swine!" Mr. Andrews said.

As he finished speaking Alec rose to his feet and poured himself out another drink. Only when he moved did Vivian relax and at last take her eyes from his face.

For a moment she dropped her head, fighting for control, striving to find her voice and to overcome the wild desire to burst into hysterical and violent sobbing.

As he walked back to the table Alec put his hand for a moment on her shoulder.

"There is one consolation, Vivian," he said gently. "They will treat your father well. You see, they want to use him."

"You are sure of that?" Vivian asked.

"I am quite sure," Alec said firmly. "It bears out our reports. The syndicate has been seen in various parts, moving about, never seeming to settle down.

"The reason is they can't make up their minds where to start. They must have got to know who your father was and they realized instantly how useful he could be to them."

"And what are you going to do now?" Mr. Andrews said with characteristic abruptness.

Alec thought for a long moment.

"I shall make for the monastery at Nyak-Tso," he said. "The monks there are friends of mine, and from there I can get some idea of where the Professor is likely to be imprisoned.

"It is bound to be somewhere in the neighborhood, because that is where the richest ores are most likely to be found. If I can once find out his exact whereabouts the rest I must leave to chance."

148

"Will you go tonight?" Mr. Andrews asked.

"Tomorrow morning," Alec replied. "We want the local authorities to think I am still looking for the Professor in the environments of the town. On no account must they realize that anything untoward has occurred. You will see to that, Andrews, of course."

Mr. Andrews nodded.

"But there is one other thing," he said, "and that is about Miss Carrow."

Alec looked at him in surprise.

"What about her?" he questioned.

"She is not safe here," Mr. Andrews went on. "You know as well as I do the things that the Kun-wa-pa Monastery can do if they choose. I was going to suggest that you should take her back in disguise to the border. I must stay here until the Doctor returns and you realize that now Tony has gone I am the only white man in the place."

"But I can't go!" Vivian ejaculated. "I can't leave now and without Daddy. Oh, Alec, you must see that you can't send me away. I must wait here for his return."

"Wait a minute," Alec said quietly. "Don't go too fast. Andrews is right, you are not safe. If they don't try to recapture you, it is quite possible that they may attempt poison or one of the other pleasant little methods. Is there no one we can trust to take you to Tatang? When is the Doctor due?"

"In another week," was the reply. "We could telephone him, of course, but he could not get here under three days."

"Then that is no use," Alec said. "We have got to think of something else. There is only one thing that we can do."

"What is that?" Vivian asked.

"You must come with me," Alec said. "At the Nyak-Tso Monastery you will be absolutely safe. They will not refuse you sanctuary if I ask it."

"And I shall be there when you find Daddy," Vivian said breathlessly. "Oh, thank you, Alec, thank you."

She stretched out both her hands toward him across the table and he took them gently in his own.

"Pray God we shall find him," he said gently.

As the eyes of the two men met above her bowed head they knew how desperate a hope it was.

CHAPTER TWELVE

"This is where we rest for the night," Alec said, shouting above the noise of the wind.

A moment later they reined in their horses at a small rough wooden hut erected in the shadow of a grey mountain rock.

Breathless and stiff from hard riding, Vivian slipped off her horse's back and followed Alec in through the rough wooden doorway.

The hut was square, one side divided off by a curiously carved partition so that the animals could be tethered and eat the pile of dried grass which hung in a net from the ceiling.

By the fireplace was a plenteous supply of fuel, and it took Alec but a few moments to get a good fire blazing.

Alec unpacked their cooking utensils from their saddle-bag and started to make the evening meal, while Vivian unrolled their sleeping bags and blankets, choosing the cleanest and least draughty corner of the hut to lay them out.

"This hut belongs to the monastery," Alec explained, as Vivian expressed her surprise that it was so clean, tidy, and convenient for travellers. "Every few days one of the monks comes here to see that everything is in readiness and to invoke a blessing on any travellers it may shelter, wherever they may be journeying."

"I call that true charity," Vivian said.

She held out her bowl for the steaming soup which Alec had prepared.

"The Abbot of the particular monastery to which we are going is one of the really great men in Tibet today," Alec said. "His knowledge is amazing, not only of the sacred works of his own religion and country, but also of what goes on in the great civilized world outside.

"He has a very good knowledge of English politics, and is one of the few Tibetans who wants to see his country freed from ignorance and barbarism."

"I shall be interested to meet him," Vivian said.

"I hope he will see you," Alec answered. "Sometimes he is in retreat for several months and may not be disturbed."

"How do you get to know all these places?" Vivian asked curiously.

Alec hesitated a moment, busy with his bowl of soup, and knitting his brows as though he were concentrating on the right words in which to reply.

"Your question is a rather difficult one to answer," he said, "because I would like to tell the truth. My associations in this land are not only because of my work—which, as you concisely informed me once in one word, is that of a spy—they are also because I have been for a long time a student and a disciple of Yoga philosophy."

Vivian raised her eyebrows in surprise.

"Are you a Yogi?" she said. "I thought they sat cross-legged in ashes, or lay on a bed of nails or something uncomfortable like that."

Alec smiled.

"That is a popular belief in the West," he said. "You see the ascetics of India gaining money by such means. But Yoga itself is a philosophy and a great faith, the foundation of all great religions whether they are Eastern or Western.

"An initiate or student, if he be acknowledged by those who really understand and know, can obtain help and services which would be denied to an outsider, however important he might be."

"And so it is as a Yogi that you are allowed to go to the monastery of Nyak-Tso," Vivian said.

"Exactly," Alec replied. "The Abbot, as it happens, is one of my oldest friends. We have been able at different times to render each other service.

"I shall be interested," he went on, "to see your reactions to a really great monastery, although I think their

151

reactions to you will be even more amusing. You will be the first white woman who has ever crossed the threshold.

"Now," he said, getting to his feet, "I think we should get some sleep. We shall have to rise with the dawn."

The wind was howling outside, making strange, almost terrifying noises as it echoed around the little hut, blowing across the wasteland of stony plains and toward the more mountainous country beyond.

"Tomorrow we start to climb," Alec had promised Vivian. "The monastery itself is not easily accessible, for they seek the higher and more refined air for their contemplation and meditations."

Alec piled up the fire, saw that their horses were comfortable, patting them and calling them by name while they rubbed their soft muzzles against him affectionately, as if they knew he was their friend and undestood their needs.

Finally he walked back to where Vivian was standing by the fire, staring into the glowing embers, daydreaming a little in the warmth.

"What are you thinking about?" he asked softly.

She turned her head swiftly towards him to find his eyes fixed upon her with the look she knew and feared.

"I was just being thankful," she said hastily, "that we have shelter for the night, and praying that Daddy is as lucky."

Alec put out his hand and took hers.

"Try not to worry," he said gently. "They will take care of your father, of that I am sure. Remember his life is very precious to them."

"Yes, I know," Vivian said. "Oh, Alec, do you think you can ever get him away?"

She said the last words desperately, clinging to his hand in supplication and appeal.

"And if I do," Alec asked, "what will you do for me?"

It was almost as if he had struck her. Vivian started, and then stood staring at him in surprise.

It was so unexpected, this question from Alec to whom she had grown used, in the last few days, to relying upon for rescue and defense from whatever dangers threatened her.

She tried to ask him what he meant, but the words would not come to her lips, and she only stood staring in wide-eyed surprise.

All her fears of him doubled and redoubled themselves in her mind.

In sudden contrition he raised her hand to his lips.

"Forgive me," he said. "I had no right to say that."

He waited a moment for some answer or response, and then softly released her hand. Vivian dropped her eyes from his face and half turned to go towards her blankets, when Alec spoke again.

"Vivian, my darling," he said hoarsely, "I love you so."

It was the cry of a desperate man, of a man tortured almost beyond endurance by his own emotions. But Vivian was deaf to everything save her own instinctive terror which made her shrink from Alec at the mere mention of love.

Every nerve in her body shrank from what she knew of Alec's brutality, of his strength, and of the determination she sensed in his relationship towards her.

She felt now when he spoke that only his self-control kept him from touching her.

She knew, as all women know, that he might at any moment seize her in his arms, and she felt that were he to do that nothing more terrifying could possibly happen to her.

It was all unreasonable and stupid, but she knew that her own thoughts were entirely beyond her control.

Without turning her head she stood trembling, feeling the tension in the air between them, knowing the look in Alec's eyes and sensing that his hands were tightly clenched at his sides.

In a voice too elaborately unconcerned to sound natural, she spoke at last.

"Did you say we had to rise at dawn?" she asked. "I hope we shall wake. It is a pity we could not have brought a servant with us."

The implication that a third person might have been welcome as a chaperon, even as an attendant, was very obvious.

Alec flushed and very slowly put his hand to his belt and drew out a small service revolver which he carried there.

"Will you take this?" he said to Vivian, holding it toward her. "I would like you to feel thoroughly protected."

153

A faint color came into her face at the sarcasm in his voice.

"I don't think I shall need it, thank you," she said.

Without another word she crept into her warm blankets.

As she lay down she knew her heart was beating rapidly, her nerves alert. She blamed herself for being drawn into a passage of words with Alec, and yet she felt he might have prevented it ever taking place.

She was acutely conscious of him lying the other side of the fire, and again in her own mind he left a chaotic impression which she could not define as hate and yet still less as liking.

She rolled over in her blankets, and under half-closed lids looked at him.

He was lying on his back, and in the flickering light of the fire she could see that his eyes were open and that he was staring at the ceiling.

Of what was he thinking, of whom was he thinking, she wondered, and in spite of his avowed love of herself she was not sure.

There was so much that was mysterious, almost enigmatical about Alec. She tried to convince herself that it was for his deeds that she feared and disliked him.

"A murderer and a spy," she told herself.

They were the words with which she had scornfully refused his proffered love, and yet she knew that her quarrel was with neither of those things.

It was the character and force of the man himself which both frightened her and yet drew her irresistibly even while she denied it.

The next day they encountered the difficulties of climbing unguided up the great mountainous heights.

Luckily they had no falling snow but the ways were dangerous, slippery, and so tortuous that even Alec once or twice found himself at a loss, and they wandered off their course.

The monasteries of Tibet are nearly all in the wildest and most inaccessible places, gripped in the teeth of a mountain or perched on the top of some mighty precipice.

Alec told Vivian that Nyak-Tso monastery had been built many centuries ago so that men who once withdrew into its isolated fastnesses need never again be disturbed by the material world.

Vivian could well believe that this was so as they climbed gorge after gorge, crossing rivers foaming over the fallen rocks. Precipices towered to right and left of them and each path seemed wilder and more dangerous, until she would not believe that they had ever been trodden by the foot of man.

All day they rode, stopping only to water their horses and drink themselves of the icy cold water which chilled their hands and seemed at the first sip to freeze their mouths and teeth.

Then on again, up and up, climbing until it became harder to breathe and the blood roared in their ears.

At last they reached a point on the gorge where snow-capped mountains and steely blue precipices seemed to bar the way to any but winged creatures and then Alec raised his hand, pointing upwards.

Vivian looked in amazement where miles away, fitting into a niche in the mountain she saw a many-windowed building of enormous height rising from terrace to terrace cut into the rock, and, indeed, part of the rock itself.

"But it is enormous," Vivian said in an awestruck voice.

"Over two thousand lamas live there," Alec replied.

"But how do they live? Where do they get their food from?" Vivian cried.

Alec, turning around in his saddle to face her, laughed at her astonished face.

"There is a narrow track which we shall join in a few minutes," he said. "It is not a very good one, but it serves the need of the monastery and will serve ours. The lamas, of course, use yaks which are more sure-footed, although we cannot complain about our ponies."

"We certainly can't," Vivian said, leaning forward to pat hers on the neck. "They have done splendidly."

"Well, we have got another three hours' climb in front of us," Alec replied.

"I feel rather nervous now I see it," Vivian said. "I don't believe I can face two thousand lamas."

"You shan't face them all at once," Alec promised.

In about an hour the path widened and wound in and out of the rocks, making it easier for the ponies, who were already suffering from the rarefied air.

Suddenly a great roar of conch shells startled Vivian, so that she nearly fell from her saddle in amazement, echoing and re-echoing down the great gorge, reverberating in a growing confusion of sound which thundered in their ears like the waves of some great ocean.

"It is all right!" Alec shouted. "They have seen us and that is their welcome."

A few moments later round the corner came a group of red-robed lamas with trumpets and pipes and prayer-flags fluttering in their hands.

Their heads were shaven, and their robes, draped artistically about them, were bright and clean and quite unlike the dirty, stained garments Vivian had seen at the Kun-wa-pa monastery.

It seemed to her that even their immobile Tibetan faces were quite different, having the sweet melancholy which comes from long solitary meditations, and the gentle smiles of men who are at peace.

Their voices were low and very musical, and in their welcome and the blessing with which they greeted Alec and Vivian she heard the famous *"Aum mani padme aum"* —Hail to the jewel in the locust—It was the sacred Buddhist mantram repeated by men, monks, praying-wheels and sacred stones all over Asia.

Little scarves inscribed with sacred writing were handed to Vivian with bows and shy smiles and on they went, the lamas crowding round Alec eagerly, asking him questions about their journey.

The monastery gates were thrown open in welcome— Vivian and Alec dismounted and were led forward into the building itself.

They went down long passages hollowed out of the rock, hundreds of doors opening on to them which seemed to Vivian like a rabbit warren.

Stone steps led off in different directions, and still the little group of lamas led them forward until finally they opened a door and showed Vivian the quarters which had been assigned to her.

It was only a small room, simply furnished with some beautiful embroidered Chinese silks, and the low Tibetan mattress which serves as a bed.

But the window, opening over the mountains and gorge below, made it an apartment more priceless than any that money could purchase in the whole world.

For a moment she felt almost giddy, looking out on to

the panorama beneath her, and then she understood completely the love of the lamas for their heights.

There was no glass in the window, but painted and carved shutters stood ready to shut out the night wind, while a huge fire burned and crackled in the stone fireplace.

"It is too lovely" Vivian said, and Alec seemed glad at her enthusiasm.

"My room is next door should you feel lonely," he said, "and now we are to pay our respects to the Abbot."

Again they set forth into the corridor, climbing many stairs and traversing endless passages until they found themselves before huge doors, ornamented and engraved with ivory and precious stones.

There was the scent of incense and the low chanting of a beautiful voice, and then the doors swung open and they stood in a long room at the end of which, seated cross-legged on a low throne, was the Abbot of Nyak-Tso.

He neither spoke nor made any gesture as they moved slowly up the long polished floor toward him, and Vivian's first impression of him was of an amazing stillness and repose.

He was an old man, for his hair was white, but his face was strangely unlined. His robe was white, and there was an embroidered stole of great beauty around his shoulders.

As they drew nearer Vivian met his eyes, and they seemed to her like bright searchlights, full of kindly yet keen observation, and she felt that under the deep quiet there was a great force and resolution about this man who ruled his monks not only as a human but as the incarnation of some divine soul.

Alec was presented formally by an attendant lama, and then, to Vivian's surprise, the Abbot spoke in English.

"Welcome, my old friend," he said to Alec. "I received your message that you were on your way, and I am indeed glad to be able to offer you hospitality, and this lady, who I understand needs sanctuary and help. Peace and mercy be yours, and what you ask of the monastery of Nyak-Tso is yours for the taking."

Bowing deeply Alec thanked the Abbot for his kindness, and then formalities were at an end, tea was brought in, and they sat down together.

To Vivian's surprise, Alec told the Abbot frankly and completely truthfully what had occurred in the past week, how she had been captured, and how the Professor was at this moment kidnapped.

The Abbot's face darkened when he spoke of Kun-wa-pa.

"The monks are a disgrace to the country," he said. "They take life and commit atrocities which horrify us to our very souls. As to your father, Miss Carrow, I have an idea that he will not be many miles from here, in the Gorge of the Wolves. It is well-known for its mineral properties, but by our powers we will look closer and you shall see for yourself."

He clapped his hands, and instantly two lamas appeared, bowing low as he gave them orders in a clear, cool voice which sounded like the far-off echoes of some chiming bell.

Vivian was to learn later that the breathing exercises of Yoga and the intonation of the sacred mantrams produced the lovely melodious voices which were characteristic of the whole monastery.

Staggering under the weight of a huge silver bowl, the lamas returned.

They placed it before the Abbot, while Vivian, after admiring the chaste relief work reminiscent more of Chinese influence than the beaten metals of India, wondered what was about to happen.

It was growing darker. The daylight was slowly fading. Before the images and sacred pictures set on the wall, small butter lamps flickered like tiny attendant glow-worms.

There was a quiet peace over everything, which made the whole scene seem unreal and dreamlike, and the faint fragrance of incense raised and steadied the mind.

Slowly monks in robes appeared bearing in their hands a large pitcher of water which they poured into the silver bowl at the Abbot's feet.

"Come nearer, my children," the Abbot said to Alec and Vivian.

They moved beside him, Vivian wonderingly, Alec with a serious face. Side by side they stood with the bowl of water at their feet.

The Abbot raised his voice. His first words came with a humming, harmonious vibration which swept around the room, whispering and echoing until it seemed to Vivian that she herself was part of the music of it.

He raised his long, thin fingers and said four words, which whispered, vibrated and echoed.

Then strangely, mysteriously, quite inexplicably to Vivian, a mist appeared and shimmered in the bowl at her feet.

She watched, fascinated, and then, like a picture on the tiny screen of a cinema, she saw far away in the bottom of the bowl a scene forming, quivering, and then steadying itself so that her vision could grasp it.

Mountains towered, a river dashed past, silver and foaming a hut appeared rough and badly constructed, not unlike the hut where she herself had spent last night.

Wide-eyed she stared at what she saw, hardly aware if from the sight of her eyes or from within her own mind she was conscious of the strange phenomenon.

The picture darkened. They were inside the hut. There was a man lying on the floor. For a moment she could not realize who it was, and then she knew and recognized her father.

His face was white and drawn, his eyes were closed, and his hand was pressed against his side as though in deep pain.

Vivian gave a little cry of horror and instantly the vision vanished, the pale mist dissolved, and there was nothing save the silver bowl and the clear crystal water in it, shimmering a little with reflected golden light.

"It was Daddy!" Vivian gasped. "Daddy! I saw him and he is ill. He is ill in that little hut by the mountains. Alec, you must go for him. Say you will go for him."

She turned beseechingly to the man at her side, clasping her hands together in her intensity, pleading with all the force of passionate unhappiness.

Not for one moment did she doubt what she had seen, not for an instant did she question the reliability of her vision.

Alec looked at her and she knew that he too had seen and understood her father's plight.

"I will go at once," he said, his voice low but steadfast.

Cool and gentle as a bell came the voice of the Abbot behind them.

"There is no time to be lost," he said. "Go, my son, and peace be with you."

* * * *

Vivian wandered restlessly up and down her small room.

Even the view through the open window with its amazing, mysterious beauty ceased to distract her mind from the gnawing anxiety she had suffered for the past forty-eight hours.

Alec had been gone all night and the day had dragged wearily hour by hour as her nerves were stretched taut with worry and fear of what might be the result of his mission.

Always before her eyes floated that strange visionary glimpse she had had of her father, suffering and apparently unattended in some desolate part of the mountains.

During the slow passing of the day she was shown some of the treasures and beauties of the monastery—the great courtyard where the men gathered at certain hours to chant, pray, or take exercise.

Here pillars, twisted and carved like bars of amber, rose to turquoise-blue roofs, weatherbeaten and mellowed to a lovely color impossible to reproduce or describe.

The cloisters which led off the courtyard were decorated and gilded with strange exotic animals, and saintly gods and goddesses before which burned many tiny lamps flickering their yellow light day and night like little guardian stars.

At noon and again at eventide the great conch shells would roar out their reverberating echoes and into the courtyard would come a seal of red, scarlet and crimson figures.

The lamas gathered together, their voices rising like some strange deep-throated melodious melody.

Vivian was allowed to watch the scene from one of the overhanging balconies shielded from the view of those below by a lattice of chaste ironwork.

It all seemed to her too amazing to be real—the heads of the lamas bowed in prayer while the richly robed chiefs of the monastery grouped themselves round the throne of the Abbot.

Yet what was even stranger than the sight itself was the deep and overwhelming atmosphere of peace, composure, and happiness which emanated from this great company.

A gentle knock at the door disturbed her agitated pacing to and fro, and when she called "Come in," a lama entered with a respectful bow, carrying a lantern.

Quietly the monk set it in a niche in the wall from where it could cast a soft golden light over the whole room, then he closed the shutters and prepared the table for the evening meal.

Vivian ate alone the inevitably buttered tea, oatmeal cakes served with a huge dab of butter on top and dried apricots, all brought to her on dishes carved and ornamented with beautiful and ancient designs.

It was a frugal but nevertheless nourishing meal and she knew that the monks had supplied her with their best.

When she had finished, a lama called her to an audience with the Abbot and she was taken through the endless corridors, not to the great hall where he had received her and Alec but to his own private sitting room.

The Tibetan carpet was of very gorgeous colorings and the Abbot himself sat at a lacquered desk, the feet and ornaments of which were of gilded wood, as was the thronelike chair in which he was seated.

All around the wall golden images almost lifesize were raised on carved pedestals and everywhere there were books—books bound in metal frames, in carved wooden covers as is the way in Tibet, and books which seemed to Vivian even in the none too bright light of the room to look peculiarly European.

She had hardly time, though, to take in her surroundings before the Abbot welcomed her with his gentle smile and a graceful gesture of his thin hands.

When she was seated before him the attendant lamas withdrew.

"I have news for you of your father, Miss Carrow," the Abbot said.

"News!" Vivian ejaculated, for this was something she had not expected. "But how? From Alec? What have you heard?"

"We have our own way of knowing these things," the Abbot said softly. "But I am afraid my news is not very good. Your father is ill, as you know already. Captain Alexander has, however, found him and managed, with our help, to procure assistance from several trustworthy men who are bringing him here."

Vivian started to her feet with excitement.

"Oh, how can I thank you?" she said. "When will they arrive?"

"They should reach the monastery when the moon is on the wane, about an hour before dawn," the Abbot said. "You will be notified immediately of their arrival, but I am afraid your father is suffering greatly."

"Has he been wounded?" Vivian asked, but the Abbot shook his head.

"Privation, cold, and dysentery, which comes from eating Tibetan meat, are worse enemies to the body than any bullet. But rest assured," he added, "that all our medical skill will be at his disposal, while our prayers are already being constantly offered on his behalf."

"Thank you. Thank you," Vivian breathed again.

"And if I may suggest it, my child," the Abbot continued, "I should rest now until your father's arrival."

But Vivian found it hard to carry out his advice. She lay down on the comfortable mattress in her room but neither rest nor sleep would come to her.

She asked herself how a sick man could be brought up those dreadful mountain roads, how Alec could contrive transport, even with the help of many men and horses.

While she asked the questions she knew she did not doubt for one moment that he would succeed, that whatever the difficulties he would overcome them, and that his indomitable will, when once he had made up his mind, was bound to have its way.

"I trust him," she told herself, "even while I am afraid of him."

Vivian was dozing fitfully when a footfall and a sharp knock awakened her instantly and she sprang from the bed and opened the door.

The lama outside beckoned her and she followed him, her heart thumping painfully as she moved swiftly down the corridor to a door at which Alec stood waiting.

Vivian held out both her hands to him in a spontaneous gesture of gladness and relief.

"Oh, my dear!" she said, and he drew her into a room.

On a raised mattress she saw her father lying, attended by two lamas, his face pale and drawn against the pillows that supported him.

"Daddy," she said with a little choking sob, and ran forward.

She fell on her knees beside him and took his hand in hers. Slowly his eyes opened and rested contentedly on her face.

"Are you all right, my darling?" he said weakly.

At the sound of his voice tears welled up into Vivian's eyes and only by a great effort of control did she stop them blinding and choking her.

"And you?" she answered. "What have they done to you?"

"I have defeated them," he said, speaking in a hoarse whisper. "At any rate for the time being."

He gave a little smile of satisfaction. One of the lamas whispered to Alec and he came up to the bedside.

"Your father must not talk too much," he said to Vivian in a low voice.

"Of course not. Let Alec tell me, Daddy. What happened?" she asked.

Gravely Alec looked down at her as she knelt beside her father, her eyes shining with unshed tears, her mouth trembling.

"The Professor gave them directions," Alec said, "which he tells me were entirely incorrect. Having no further use for him they left him without food in a desolate part of the mountains miles from any human beings, or so they thought, and, what was worse, without any chance of being found or rescued.

"He only knew that when they had discovered the trick he had played on them there was every likelihood of their returning to murder him."

"Daddy, why must you be so brave?" Vivian cried. "Your life is so much more precious than all the gold mines in the world."

The Professor opened his eyes again and made a brave attempt to smile at her, and Vivian dropped her cheek against his hand, kissing it and letting the tears flow from her eyes while her face was hidden.

"You must let him sleep," Alec said quietly.

He helped her to her feet and led her gently from the room. Outside the door she put her hands pleadingly on his arm, holding on to it tightly and agonizingly.

"Is he really ill?" she said. "He isn't dying? Tell me, I must know. Tell me the truth."

Alec did not speak.

"Don't lie to me," she begged. "Can't you realize he is the only person and the only thing I have in the whole world?"

"He is very ill," Alec said gravely.

"Can't we get doctors? Can't we get somebody to do something?" Vivian said wildly.

"There is no one in the whole country who knows more about medicine than the lamas in this monastery," Alec replied. "You must trust them. But at the same time even they cannot perform miracles. Your father has been without food and without heat for nearly three days. He is not a young man, we can only hope and pray."

Vivian passed her hand in front of her eyes, and then quite calmly, and with an almost dignified composure, she said:

"I shall sit with him now while he sleeps."

"You had much better rest yourself," Alec answered. "You cannot help him at the moment."

But Vivian looked at him, and he saw that her mind was made up. No arguments would move her.

She felt that her place was by her father's side and Alec, for once defeated and without a word of protest, opened the door so that she might pass back into the sick-room.

* * * *

Once or twice during the night the Professor asked weakly for water, otherwise the long hours passed uneventfully.

Vivian did not feel especially tired during her long vigil.

It seemed, indeed, to her that she must pour all her vitality out of herself in a steady wave toward her father, that by a sheer effort of will she could revive and sustain him.

Her concentration was so great that at times she felt that she could actually sense the vibrations which joined her with the one she loved.

With the dawn the Professor seemed to be sleeping a little easier.

Yet the pallor of his face and the faintness of his breathing made Vivian fear that he was sinking rather than growing in strength.

During the night Alec came into the room to look at the sick man.

He did not speak to Vivian, but his hand rested on her shoulder, and almost gratefully she glanced up at him with a faint smile, feeling for once that they were united in understanding and a mutual sympathy.

With the dawn came far-off echoes of the conch shells calling the monks to prayer in the great courtyard, and the attendant lamas withdrew silently from the sickroom.

When they had gone Vivian walked across the room and opened wide the shutters which barred the window.

The bright sun, already throwing dazzling fingers across the paling sky, glimmered on the white tops of the surrounding mountains.

To Vivian, high above the world, there was in this entranced silence an ecstasy of mind and spirit which transcended all, even the bitterness of earthly sorrows.

Here one could believe in miracles, one could have faith both in God and man.

As Vivian turned back to the bedside of her father she saw that his eyes were open and with a tender smile she said gently:

"Please get well, darling. I love you so."

During the morning the Abbot himself visited the sick man, giving him a special blessing and bringing a small, yet exquisitely beautiful image of the Goddess of Health.

It was arranged with tender care by the Professor's side, and again and again his eyes rested on it in appreciation.

Alec insisted on Vivian leaving her father and lying down.

He led her, protesting, to her own bedroom and sternly commanded her to sleep.

"But I am not tired," she said. "And I want to be with him."

"I let you have your way last night," he answered. "It is my turn now. I will stay with him for the next few hours and if there is the slightest change or any alteration in his health, I promise you I will call you immediately."

"Do you swear it?" Vivian said, looking at him anxiously, as though she doubted his word.

"Have you ever known me to fail you?" he said abruptly, but very seriously.

For once she felt ashamed of her own doubts of him.

She dropped her eyes from his face and moved into her own room.

"I am always afraid you will do what you think best for me, and not what I want done," she said easily, to pass off an awkward moment.

"One day, perhaps, the two will be synonymous," Alec replied, and unexpectedly Vivian laughed.

"It would be a change, wouldn't it?" she said.

Just for a moment they were two ordinary young people, smiling at each other.

Then the moment passed and once again the deep cloud of anxiety and fear descended on them both, so that Vivian, turning wearily towards her bedroom said:

"You promise, then. Come for me when he wakes, even if it is only for a few minutes."

"I promise," Alec answered, and shut the door gently.

Vivian had overrated her strength.

The moment she lay down sleep took her into its deep embrace, but even as she sank into the realms of deep unconsciousness she felt a vague resentment that once again Alec had been right and that she had indeed needed rest.

When she took up her vigil again at her father's side he opened his eyes and moved his hand very weakly towards her.

She took it in both of hers, then, bending low, kissed him lightly on the forehead. Very slowly his lips moved.

She had to bend her head still further to hear the barely articulate words which came in a whisper.

"God bless you, my dear," he said.

Then wearily he closed his eyes again and passed into a deep unconsciousness.

Hours passed and Vivian longed for Alec's return that she might ask him to question the lamas.

She was afraid of her father's stillness, but Alec was a long time coming, and Vivian felt almost resentful at his lack of attention.

Finally, when she was just making up her mind to send for him, he appeared. He walked straight across the room to her side and said in a low voice:

"I want you to come with me to see the Abbot."

In silence, for fear of disturbing her father, Vivian followed him from the room.

In the doorway Alec spoke to the two attendant lamas, and then they passed side by side down the long corridors until they came to the doors which led to the Abbot's private apartments.

Here they were met by a monk and escorted into his presence.

The Abbot was seated at his desk, but he rose courteously as Vivian entered. A chair was drawn up for her and the inevitable bowl of tea placed by her side.

Alec spoke first.

"I have told Miss Carrow nothing as yet," he said. His voice sounded strangely disturbed, so that Vivian looked at him in surprise.

"What has happened?" she asked anxiously.

"Captain Alexander has asked me to explain to you the very difficult position we are in," the Abbot said in his low, musical voice. "News has just been brought to us that the Russians who abducted your father have discovered the trick he played on them; and have also found that he himself has escaped their vengeance.

"They have roused a portion of the countryside and have also allied themselves with the fighting monks of the Kun-wa-pa Monastery, and are on their way here to demand that your father be given up to them and also any other foreigners within these walls."

"Are they trying to frighten us?" Vivian asked. "After all, they will stand little chance against the thousands of men in this stronghold."

"I am afraid you don't understand, Miss Carrow," the Abbot said gently. "You see, I and the monks under my charge follow the true faith and teaching of the great Lord Buddha. We do not fight or take life in any form.

Vivian started to her feet.

"Then you mean," she said in horror, "that you will give us up to these devils? Oh, you can't mean it! My father is ill! He is dying!

"Hush, my child," the Abbot said gently. "Listen to what Captain Alexander suggests."

"The Abbot," Alec said, speaking quickly and decisively, "has offered us horses and attendants for some part of our journey. We must leave at once and make for the Kampa Pass.

"It is supposed to be closed in winter, but people have

167

been known to enter Tibet in this way, and there is a chance, although it is a desperate one, that we can get through and find ourselves in Sikkim."

"But Daddy. How can we move Daddy?" Vivian asked, her eyes fixed on Alec's face.

"The Abbot will protect the Professor while he is ill against the invaders," Alec said. "When he is well again he cannot, of course, answer for your father's safety. Then it will be up to me to help him to escape.

"But while he is ill he is under the medical charge of the monastery and they will not dare to move him. But for you the Abbot can give no such surety, and it is imperative that you leave here tonight."

"And you think," Vivian asked, "that I would go now and leave my father to such a fate? A thousand times no! If we die, we will die together."

"But don't you understand," Alec said urgently, "that you and I will be taken prisoners by these people? They cannot be refused entrance if they use violence, and if they know we are here nothing will stop them breaking and battering their way into the monastery."

"Save yourself then," Vivian said scornfully. "I, personally, would rather die than abandon my father at such a time."

"You can do no good by staying, Miss Carrow," the Abbot said.

But Vivian turned to him with her chin high and her eyes blazing with determination.

"You have been very kind," she said, "and I am more than grateful for your hospitality both to me and to my father. But nothing would make me leave him now."

She bowed, and, without waiting for Alec, walked towards the door.

On the threshold she turned back and saw that he was speaking with the Abbot, and without another word or look she passed from the Abbot's apartments and hurried back to her father.

In the sickroom again she waved the attendant lamas to one side and seated herself by the bed. She felt no fear of her decision, she only knew that whatever happened she must stay.

Her father would never have abandoned her, and there was no other course open to her.

She could not visualize what the future might hold, but she knew that nothing would alter her determination.

She vaguely sensed that in a few moments Alec would follow her and try to argue or coerce her into doing what he wanted. She told herself that his words would be of no avail this time.

"Do you think I would leave you, darling?" she whispered beneath her breath as she watched her father.

The tears came to her eyes as she realized how ill and weak he was. If they were to wait for him to get well they would have to wait a long time.

To her surprise, Alec did not follow her. Nearly an hour passed and she heard the trumpets blaring in a distant part of the monastery which told the monks that their supper was ready.

One of the lamas left the room and then returned about five minutes later carrying a tray burdened with supper dishes. He was followed by Alec.

"I thought you would like your food here," he said, "rather than in your own room."

His voice was kind and unalarming, and instantly Vivian experienced a feeling of relief. So he was not going to argue or to plead with her. He had accepted her decision. Gratefully she answered:

"Thank you."

The lama placed the tray of silver and carved dishes at her side.

Alec, taking up the teabowl, carried it over to the fireplace to fill it from the huge kettle of stewing tea which had been kept ready all day, both for the patient and his attendants.

Carrying the steaming bowl in both his hands, he brought it back to her.

"Are you tired?" he said kindly, speaking in a very low voice.

Vivian shook her head.

"Not particularly," she said, "but I am very thirsty."

Alec held out the bowl towards her, and she took it with both hands.

"This will do you good," he said.

She sipped it, and the liquid seemed to fortify and warm her as it slipped easily down her dry throat.

She tipped the bowl again toward her mouth and as

169

she did so a strange suspicion began to form itself in her mind.

Why was Alec so attentive? Why had he himself brought her the tea? She checked the impulse to drink. Her eyes met Alec's, and as if he instantly knew her thoughts he moved swiftly.

Before she could cry out or protest, he had seized the teabowl in one hand while his other hand fastened around her shoulders in a grip of iron.

Tipping the bowl he forced the contents searingly down her throat.

She struggled, an overwhelming emotion of anger and impotency choking her, and then as her hands came out to ward him off a sudden desperate darkness descended upon her.

She fought against the oblivion which made her limbs feel as heavy as lead, which subdued her will and smothered her voice when she would have cried out.

The room spun round her, darkness descended.

As she fell forward into unconsciousness Vivian saw Alec's eyes, somber, dark, bitterly triumphant.

CHAPTER THIRTEEN

Vivian was conscious of movement, and of strong arms holding her firmly and giving her a sense of security which penetrated her drowsiness.

Then gradually her brain began to take control over her senses. She opened her eyes, but for a moment she was still too hazy and too drugged to grasp reality.

Her head was against Alec's shoulder and she could see the firm line of his chin as he looked beyond her, guiding his horse while she lay across the bow of his saddle.

For a few seconds she lay motionless, rocked like a baby in the cradle of his arms, and then she realized that the mountains were gone.

All around them lay nothing but the flat plain, parched and barren of any relief either of vegetation or formation.

Then she remembered. With a little cry she strove to free herself from Alec's encircling arm.

Without a word, he reined in his horse, stopped, and let her slide gently to the ground.

Then he dismounted, and she stood staring about her, looking towards another horse which followed and upon which was mounted a red-robed lama.

It took Vivian some seconds before she could control her voice, and then it came hoarsely from her throat.

"Why have you brought me here?" she demanded. "What have you done? I am going back to Daddy."

She stood quivering all over, her hands clenched at her sides, her head thrown back.

They must have ridden all night, she thought swiftly, for already the sun had risen in the heavens.

There was no sign of the amazing heights wherein the monastery was situated, and the rarefied air had been replaced by the dry and more normal atmosphere of the lower plains.

"My dear," Alec said, speaking very kindly. "You cannot return to your father now."

"But I will," Vivian stormed. "You had no right to behave like this, to drug me and bring me here. He is in danger, he is dying. Do you suppose I want to be saved in such circumstances?"

Alec put out his hand and placed it gently on Vivian's shoulder.

"Your father," he said, his voice low and direct, "was not alive when we left the monastery last night."

"I don't believe you," Vivian said.

For a moment the meaning of his communication did not sink into full realization in her mind.

"It is true," Alec went on. "When you spoke to the Abbot last night he knew then, as I did, that the Professor would not last until the dawn. I hoped to spare you the pain of knowing that the end was inevitable.

"But when you refused to leave your father's side I realized that you would jeopardize, however brief the delay, your own life and mine, and so I was forced to take matters into my own hands."

"How dared you?" Vivian said fiercely. "What right had you to deny me those last hours with Daddy? Now he has gone do you think I care for my own safety? Do you think I will let you take care of me? You a murderer and a spy.

"I don't believe you," she cried suddenly hysterical. "He isn't dead. You are telling me this to get me away."

"I swear to you that it is true," Alec said solemnly. He stood immobile, solid and stalwart under the storm of Vivian's words.

"I hate you, I hate you!" she cried. "I refuse to listen. I will go back to the monastery and find out the truth for myself."

Wildly, madly, hardly aware of what she was doing she made an impulsive dash at Alec's horse. But before she could reach the bridle, with the quickness of a man used to swift action, Alec caught her hands and held them in his.

"Let me go, let me go!" she cried, struggling and fighting with him, mad with misery and unhappiness.

"Stop!" Alec said severely.

He spoke in the abrupt commanding tone he had used on that long journey from the Kun-wa-pa Monastery, the voice which had spurred her on against the weakness of her own flesh.

Now it arrested her violent struggles and forced her to concentrate.

"I don't believe you," she said a moment later.

But her voice was less wild and her tone lacked conviction.

"Yes, you do," Alec replied gently.

"Why should I trust your word?" Vivian flashed back, defying him while her eyes dared not meet his.

Her hands were still gripped and imprisoned but she leaned away from him as far as she could.

"We must go on," Alec said. "This is no time for lingering or for conversation."

"I won't go," Vivian said stubbornly. "I will stay here and die rather than be taken on against my will by a murderer."

"Listen to me," Alec said, suddenly releasing her hands, and instead gripped both her shoulders tightly, almost cruelly. "You have called me that once too often. I should have told you the truth a long time ago, but it seemed unnecessary. Dhilangi was killed by my servant.

"He had abducted and raped his betrothed, and the man waited, promising revenge, even if his chance did not come for many years.

"When the opportunity occurred, he took it, but at what proved a most inconvenient moment for the British Government should the full facts of the case have been revealed.

"As my servant there would have been every reason to suspect that the assassination of Dhilangi was one of political expediency rather than the mere individual justice meted out by man to man.

"Dhilangi was such a devil that I swore to myself that I would never give my servant up to justice while he lived. He died aboard the *Corinthia* and a full confession, dictated to me, is in the hands of the authorities. That is all. There is no more for me to say."

He took his hands from Vivian's shoulder as abruptly as he had put them there.

Without waiting for her to speak he beckoned to the lama who had been waiting some way behind them, and when the man rode up he spoke swiftly to him in Tibetan.

The monk dismounted, and still without a word Alec helped Vivian into the saddle and then the two men said farewell, the lama raised his hand in a blessing.

A few minutes later Vivian and Alec were galloping across the plain, while behind them the small red-robed figure dwindled into the distance as he strode off rapidly in the direction from which they had come.

As they galloped forward, Vivian, silent and dazed, began to feel the full realization of her father's loss.

She did not cry, only an aching agony seemed to settle in her heart, making her crave for the relief of tears.

On and on they traveled until in the early afternoon she saw the mountains in front of them, and the plain began to slope gradually upwards.

On the Tibetan side of the Himalayas there is little snow, but the valley which leads up to the Kampa Pass is formed by precipitous cliffs bounded on the north and south by the overshadowing mountain ranges.

They rode all day without speaking, except when Alec directed Vivian to keep behind him, or suggested that she might find such and such a path easier going.

When the intense cold started to replace the burning heat of the sun, Alec drew up his horse for a moment and handed Vivian a yakskin coat.

"Thank you," she said.

She put her arms through the wide sleeves and pulled the hood low over her face so that she was protected from the biting wind.

Without another word Alec, having wrapped himself in a similar manner, led the way forward.

Vivian's heart and soul were crying out to her father, finding it hard to believe that he had indeed left her, and that she would never see him again.

Yet she was all the time conscious of her silent companion, aware for the first time in her life of what utter loneliness could mean.

They climbed higher and higher, passing a great glacier, the horses beginning to breathe with difficulty, and finding the paths increasingly hard to negotiate.

At last, when Vivian felt she could go no farther, when exhaustion and cold had numbed and paralyzed her limbs until there was practically no feeling left, they paused on a small plateau thousands of feet above sea level, on which there was built a small hut.

Alec dismounted and led the way to the rough door. There were huge chinks in the wall, and the wind played in and out of them, but at least it was shelter.

Vivian unloaded the animals while Alec sought for fuel, and after several ineffectual attempts he managed to get the fire going.

Hot tea revived them both, and when at last she was beginning to thaw, Vivian looked up to find his eyes resting upon her in silent sympathy.

"I am sorry," she said, "for the way I behaved this morning."

"Please don't be," Alec said hastily, with a note of embarrassment in his voice. "I know how you must feel, but I had to get you away."

"It was very good of you," Vivian said, "but I cannot feel grateful as yet. When I know what this terrible country has done to Daddy, I can feel no interest in my own future."

"Not at the moment," Alec said, "but later, perhaps. The most precious thing of all, if we only realize it, is life."

Vivian dropped her head, so that he could not see the tears in her eyes.

Until they were safe, until they had escaped, she told herself, she must not relax her control.

"We are near the top," Alec said. "Tomorrow by midday we should reach the Pass."

"And then?" Vivian said, trying to take an interest in his plans.

"And then," he went on, "we reach the worst part of our journey. We shall encounter snow, though how deep and whether impassable or not, I don't know."

* * * *

Vivian was to remember his words the next day when they came to the Pass. The snow was deep in the gorge which led directly into a small mountain-surrounded valley.

The horses would not struggle through it unless led, and Vivian and Alec started to walk, at each step sinking deeper and deeper, until it required all their energy to move one step forward, dragging one buried leg after the other.

The dark clouds passed, and the sun started to shine brilliantly, and scorchingly, and Alec searched in his saddle-pack and found some dark glasses which he held out to Vivian.

"Put these on," he commanded.

She did as she was told, and again they plunged forward, the horses whimpering with fear as the snow seemed to grow deeper and deeper.

It took them between two and three hours to traverse a small valley, and to climb up the other side, coaxing and dragging the animals up a path slippery with ice.

The road lay deeply buried, and they had to guess their way. Once Alec's horse slipped and fell, and only in desperate plunging did it regain its feet.

On and on they struggled, Vivian following in Alec's footsteps, feeling sometimes that she would sooner give in and sink into the soft snow-drifts rather than struggle another step forward.

Finally, when the light began to fade, she became anxious. Supposing they could find nowhere to shelter for the night? She knew the dangers of lying out.

Intense cold had come with the sinking of the sun, though here they were spared the bitter, cruel winds of Tibet, but they had no tent with them, and she knew that unless they could find shelter neither of them would be alive in the morning.

Once in the distance she heard the howl of a wolf, and she shivered to think what their fate might be if they did not soon strike one of the huts erected for travellers.

Alec seemed to be going slower, and though she was grateful it did not diminish her anxiety.

When finally through the gathering dusk she suddenly espied ahead the rough outline of a wooden hut, nestling against the dark rocks, she gave a cry of joy.

"Shelter!" she cried to Alec.

He stared around as though he could not see it, and so

overjoyed was she that she plunged forward into the snow, passing Alec and his horse and arriving as joyously at the dilapidated snow-covered hut as at a luxurious hotel.

She led her horse in through the creaking door, and tied it up in the corner, groping her way in the darkness.

"I was getting anxious," she said conversationally, as Alec entered.

"Will you take my horse?" he said.

"Of course," she answered.

She took the bridle in her hand, tethering the animal beside her own.

"It is getting very dark," she said as she finished. "Hurry up with the fire."

Then to her surprise she saw that Alec had not moved.

He stood just where she had left him, inside the door of the hut, and from where she stood she could see him silhouetted against the open door and the white snow outside.

"What is it, Alec?" she asked.

Something in his attitude frightened her. He did not answer, and she sped forward.

"What is it?" she cried. "Are you ill?"

As she came near him, he put out his hand and took hers.

Even in the feel of his fingers there was something unusual, a groping, hesitant movement which was so unlike Alec that again Vivian cried out to him.

"Tell me what it is, Alec! You must tell me!"

Slowly, through cracked lips, he answered:

"I am blind."

CHAPTER FOURTEEN

A storm broke with extraordinary violence.

The thunder was almost deafening, the lightning in sharp piercing flashes through the chinks in the roughly built hut illuminated the interior revealing Alec lying with bandaged eyes beside the flickering smoky fire.

Vivian, shivering beneath her blankets, wondered if the roof would stand the torrential sleet.

Every now and then she was forced to move her position so that the dripping water did not splash her face.

She knew that Alec was not asleep and that he was in continual pain. She had prepared their scanty supper and forced him to eat, putting everything into his hands as if he were a child.

Only now, when they had said good night, could she begin to think of what he must have suffered the whole long day in the glare and brilliance of the sun on the snow.

She knew how terrible snow blindness can be. She had seen strong men break down and weep, behaving like frightened children when they could no longer see.

The agony of irritated streaming eyes made them lose their strength and determination.

When she realized what had happened to Alec she had said:

"Why didn't you tell me there was only one pair of glasses? You must have been crazy to attempt to travel without them."

He did not try to answer her reproaches.

"I shall be all right in the morning," he said, trying to speak cheerfully.

But Vivian, as she fetched snow from outside with which to bathe his eyes, felt that it was doubtful.

Unfortunately, they had nothing medical with them which could be of the slightest use.

So she had to content herself with putting cool pads over his eyes and binding them on with her own white linen handkerchief.

It seemed strange to be ministering to Alec.

She had grown used to depending on him to do everything for her in whatever circumstances they found themselves.

When she finally piled up the fire for the night and guided him to his blankets which she had arranged in a dry place, she felt almost shy of this alteration of their roles.

"Are you all right?" she asked. "There is nothing else you want?"

"Thank you so much, Vivian," Alec answered. "I am so sorry to be such a nuisance."

There was an overwhelming pathos in his helpless humility.

The horses kept champing and whinnying with fear at every flash of lightning so it was impossible to sleep, and Vivian lay for a long time looking into the glowing embers of the fire.

She tried not to let the thought of the morrow frighten her, although how they would fare with Alec blinded and a fresh fall of snow blocking their path she had no idea.

The thought of her father came to her, and somehow instead of the agony she expected to overwhelm her she felt sure that he was quite near, giving her new courage and hope.

The impression was so strong that she felt almost that she could speak to him and stretch out her hand in welcome and affection.

"What is death?" she asked herself.

Then she knew that there was no such thing. Her father was alive, whatever had happened to his body in the monastery of Nyak-Tso.

His love for her and hers for him was a real and continuous thing which separation could never quench, and she knew she was nearer in spirit to him than she had ever been in her life before.

"Daddy," she murmured once or twice, and with a faint smile on her lips she finally fell asleep.

Morning came, but Vivian knew it only by the luminous hands on her wrist-watch, for no light came to waken her.

"It is seven o'clock," she said to Alec.

He sat up, letting his blankets fall from him and raising his hands to his bandaged eyes.

"Good heavens!" he said. "How awful! We ought to have been off at least two hours ago."

"But it is still dark," Vivian said.

Alec took off the bandages from his eyes.

"Is it really?"

He wiped his eyes. "I can't see," he said at last.

"Can't you see anything at all?" Vivian questioned. "It is dark here, but I can see the horses and you as a vague outline. It must be the snow."

"I can't see anything at all," Alec said despairingly. "Oh, my God, what are we going to do?"

Vivian tried to open the door and at last, after struggling with all her strength, she managed to get it open a few inches.

"It is snowing hard," she announced a moment later. "I can't see a yard ahead."

"Then we could not have travelled anyway," Alec said with relief in his voice.

"It would be quite impossible," Vivian answered.

She came back into the room and piled up the fire.

"You must put the bandages back at once," she said in a brisk tone. "If you save your eyes today they will be all right tomorrow. Wait a minute. I will get some fresh snow to moisten the pads."

She opened the door a few inches and then returned to place the small pads of soaked wool on Alec's eyes and bandaged them tightly round his head.

The feel of his thick hair under her fingers, his submissive attitude as he let her arrange the pads on his eyes, gave her a new and strange sensation.

"I like nursing him," she thought. "I suppose every

180

woman enjoys it at heart. It allows one to boss even the strongest and most self-sufficient men."

His quiet 'Thank you' as she finished gave her a thrill.

Here was a very different Alec from the one she had known before. This was no commanding, forceful man from whom she shrank in terror.

Instead, it was just someone dependent on her, someone who would have been utterly helpless and abandoned had she not been with him.

"We must not be too greedy over our meals today," she said, as she mixed some barley flour and boiled a cauldron of tea.

"How much is there left?" Alec asked sharply.

"Oh, enough for today and tomorrow, if we are not too hungry," she replied.

But it gave her much satisfaction a few minutes later to give him by far the larger share of their meager breakfast and to refill his bowl of tea while hers remained empty.

Through the long day that followed they sat talking round the fire, discussing, it seemed to Vivian, everything in the world save their own plight and predicament.

Never before had she realized what an interesting companion Alec could be. He told her tales of his adventures in strange parts of the world.

He told her of the exploits of men of all nationalities.

Every now and then he introduced a human and tender note into his reminiscences which made her glance at him in surprise as if she could not understand this new aspect of the man she had feared and hated.

"I have never understood women," he said later, when Vivian's watch told them that the afternoon was drawing to a close. "My mother died when I was born and I was brought up by my father in an old castle in Scotland miles from any companions of my own age and knowing only the Gaelic-speaking fishermen who lived on the estate."

"But you must have known heaps of women in your life," Vivian said, "and fallen in and out of love hundreds of times."

"I have never loved anyone until I met you," Alec said soberly.

For the first time his mention of love did not startle Vivian. There was nothing frightening in the quiet, still figure with bandaged eyes sitting helplessly by her side.

"I do not see how you could be in love with me that is, when you first said you were," she answered. "After all, you knew, and still know for that matter, very little about me."

"I knew it the first moment I saw you," Alec said.

Something vital in his voice sent a strange thrill through her body.

"When I saw you in the Casino two days before we met that awful night in the summerhouse," he went on. "I knew that you were the only woman who could ever matter in my life."

"How could you know that?" she asked.

"Haven't you felt out here, that such things are ordained," he enquired. "When I saw your face, it was as if I had seen it before in a dream, in another life, who knows?"

There was a pause.

"Only one difference," he went on. "You were lovelier, much, much more lovelier than I remembered."

Vivian felt herself tremble but it was not with fear.

"I love everything about you," Alec said very quietly. "I love your eyes, your little straight nose, your smile and the wonderful light in your hair."

He drew a deep breath.

"But I also love your courage, and the way you put up your chin when you are defying me and the little sob in your voice when you are unhappy."

He was silent but Vivian could not speak. She could only feel herself drawn and entranced by the deep note in his voice.

"We can't escape each other, my darling," he said. "We belong to each other. You and I."

Vivian's heart was beating and she was conscious that she was trembling a little, and yet strangely enough she did not wish to run away.

She wanted to know more, to listen to that voice with its deep, vibrating intonation.

Only when Alec did not speak did a sudden shyness make her rise and move about the hut, pretending as an excuse that she was seeing to one of the horses.

As she patted their necks, she hid for a moment her burning cheeks against their rough hair.

182

Something strange was happening to her, something she had never experienced before.

There was a warmth and a glow in her heart, and a gladness for which she would not ask herself the explanation.

At eight o'clock they ate again, and then once more Vivian arranged the blankets for Alec and guided him to them.

"Sleep well," she said lightly, "for we must get off at dawn."

In answer he raised her hand to his lips, groping for it and then holding it firmly in his strong clasp.

"I hate being helpless," he said.

He could not see the suspicious brightness of Vivian's eyes or the sudden trembling of her lips as he bent his head over her hand.

"Good night," she said a few moments later, and then there was complete silence in the hut.

They were both awakened two hours later by the noise of some animal prowling around outside. The horses started to plunge about in a frightened manner.

Suddenly there was a hideous, ear shattering howl, which seemed almost to be inside the hut.

It was so terrifying that without thinking, driven by an uncontrollable fear, Vivian sprang across the hut and threw herself against Alec.

She felt his arms go around her and hid her face against his shoulder.

"Is . . . it . . . a wolf," she whispered, "will it . . . hurt us?"

He held her closer and pulled the blankets that covered him over them both.

"It is more likely to be a snow leopard," he answered.

"What . . . shall we . . . do?" Vivian asked.

Her voice trembled. There was something uncanny and terrifying in being sniffed at by some ferocious wild beast.

"It won't do us any harm," Alec replied, "and I don't want to waste a bullet by firing to scare it away."

"It . . . can't get inside the . . . hut?" Vivian asked.

"I will protect you!"

There was something in Alec's voice which made her raise her face from his shoulder. And then, she was not certain how it happened, his mouth came down on hers.

Just for a moment she stiffened, then suddenly something wonderful seemed to streak through her body like a flash of lightning.

It was so marvelous, so unlike any sensation she had ever known before that her lips could only cling to his and she could no longer think.

She felt as if she came alive, that her whole being pulsated with a rapture that was inexpressible.

Finally as she quivered against him with the intensity of her feelings he raised his head.

"My darling—my precious, my brave little love," he said unsteadily and then he was kissing her again.

Kissing until she felt as if they were carried to the peaks of the snowy mountains on the wings of song.

"I love you—oh, my darling, how I love you," Alec said.

And at last Vivian could answer him.

"I didn't . . . know . . . I didn't understand . . ." she murmured.

"What didn't you understand, my sweet?" he asked.

"That . . . I wanted . . . you," she answered. "To be . . . close . . . to you."

"I wanted you so desperately," he replied. "And you could not escape—you are mine!"

She stayed in his arms all night, safe and at peace.

It was almost as if she had found her way home after a long long jorney.

"It is morning," she heard Alec say when she was still dozing and moved to fling wide the door.

A world of virgin white met her eyes under a sky clear and cloudless up which the first golden rays of the rising sun were climbing.

"It is a lovely day," she cried out joyously.

She turned to find Alec standing upright, the bandage in his hand.

"I am still blind," he said.

For a moment Vivian, too, felt her heart sink, but she fought back the exclamation of horror which came to her lips.

"Never mind," she answered. "I can lead you. We are through the Pass now and we will find the way down somehow."

"Do you think you can?" Alec asked.

"Of course I can," Vivian replied. "We have got to.

There is only a small breakfast for both of us and I for one am going to be very hungry by dinnertime."

She prepared the tea and mixed the last remaining flour into a form of dough-cake.

"Here you are," she said to Alec. "That is your share."

He put out his hand and took hers so swiftly that she was surprised at the accuracy of his movement.

"If this is my share," he said, "show me yours."

"It is over there," Vivian said, lying.

"That is not true," Alec answered. "Listen, my darling one, I may be blind, but I am not going to let you bully me. You will eat this at once."

He forced her, against her laughing protests, to eat the unsavoury cake.

"But I want to share it," Vivian said, struggling.

"You were not allowing me the opportunity of doing that," he said grimly. "Oh, my precious love, do you think I don't worship you for doing such a thing?"

Vivian blushed at the tone of his voice, and then eluding his compelling hands she poured out the tea from the tiny cauldron.

"I really have halved this," she said, and put the bowl into Alec's hands.

Ten minutes later they were ready to start, and only then, as she looked out on the white mountainside, did Vivian realize a terrifying thing.

The path lay deep buried in the snow. Huge drifts had been blown about during the night and they had no way of knowing where lay a precipice, gorge, or firm foothold.

In this part of the world if either of them fell into a crevass, rescue, especially with one of the party maimed, would be impossible.

She stood looking for a long time before she spoke, and then in a voice despondent and low she said to Alec:

"I can't see the road. It is completely covered."

Alec stood still. He knew even better than Vivian that if the treacherous, twisting, Himalayan paths are once completely buried there is little hope.

For the first time since they had left the monastery Vivian felt that both God and man had abandoned her.

To remain meant starvation, to go forward meant death. There was no food and not the slightest hope of anyone coming to their rescue.

"We are finished," she said bitterly.

Suddenly her control vanished, and overcome by emotion she hid her face with its blinding tears against his shoulder.

"Hush, hush, my darling," he said, putting his arms around her and holding her slim body, racked by sobs, closely to him.

"I don't want to die!" Vivian wept.

Alec tightened the grip of his arms around her shoulders.

"You shan't," he said. "We have got so far, we shall succeed. Look out again and tell me exactly what you see —explain the formation of the rocks. There must be some solution."

Instantly Vivian obeyed the command in his voice.

Finding new courage, she wiped her eyes with her hand and turned from Alec's embrace toward the open door again.

The rising sun glittered on her wet lashes, blinding her for a moment, and then she looked about her, desperately anxious, trying to find words to explain clearly to Alec all she could see.

She was ashamed of her lack of self-control and her first words she tried to make light, but her voice was hoarse.

"You were right," she said, "it was a snow leopard in the night. He has left his footprints all round the hut and then he was gone zigzagging down the mountain. He has gone a long way."

"They are extraordinary animals," Alec answered, trying also to speak as lightly. "The natives believe they have super-natural powers because they can walk on top of the snow without sinking into it."

"Can they?" Vivian said.

She looked around, formulating in her mind how high the hut would be above the hidden path.

Suddenly, way back in her mind, memory began to stir.

Then she gave a cry which startled Alec, making him give an instinctive movement towards her as if to protect her.

"Alec!" she cried. "Tell me, tell me quickly—when a snow leopard walks on top of the snow does he follow the road beneath?"

Alec gripped her arm so tightly that it was painful.

"I have always heard so. Naturalists attribute it to some acute sense of smell."

"Then we are saved," Vivian cried. "We are saved, Alec! The snow-leopard's track lies before us, zigzagging just in the way that the path is most likely to do, and the oracle at Chumbi told me I must follow in the steps of the snow leopard if I would find life and . . ."

Her voice ceased.

She was suddenly conscious of her tear-stained face, radiant with relief and hope, of Alec standing beside her, his hand gripping her arm, his bandaged face turned towards her.

She stood quivering, savouring the utter ecstasy of the moment.

Then Alec, still tense, asked her a question.

"You would find life," he said, "and what else?"

His voice vibrated, and drew her irresistibly until glorious, expansive, and overwhelming as the sun itself, love took her into its keeping.

Throwing her arms around him, her face turned up to his, Vivian's voice rang out, happy and triumphant.

"And love and hope, darling," she replied.

Then there was only the wonder of his lips on hers and the glory of the sunshine.

THE END OR
THE BEGINNING

The bungalow above Darjeeling was surrounded by rhododendrons and azaleas, their colors crimson, orange, white, mauve and scarlet like a glorious rainbow which had fallen from the sky.

Beyond the snowy peaks of the Himalayas gleamed white in the sunlight which was gradually fading in a blaze of glory into the sable of the encroaching night.

Vivian came out onto the verandah to stand looking at the beauty of it—then there was a footstep behind her and Alec joined her.

"It's so unbelievably beautiful!" she said.

"And so are you, my wonderful darling!"

He put his arms around her and she laid her head against his shoulder in a confiding gesture like that of a trusting child.

"You are not too tired, my precious?" he asked.

"I was just going to ask you the same question."

"I have never felt so well—or so happy!"

Vivian drew in a deep breath of relief and happiness.

They had been married at noon in the little English Church in the town, and after a meal with the British High Commissioner they had ridden up the twisting narrow paths to the bungalow which Alec had been lent for their honeymoon.

It was small but very comfortable and there were two servants to look after them.

"How soon will you marry me?" Alec had asked when a week after they had reached safety he had recovered his sight.

It had been for Vivian a week of desperate anxiety and even though she herself was weak with exhaustion she could think of nothing but Alec.

Now that she had acknowledged that she loved him she knew she wanted to look after him; to nurse him and tend him as if he was more like her son than her lover.

And yet every day the effect he had on her became more intense, more vivid, more overwhelming.

He had only to touch her to make her quiver with strange sensations she had never known before. She had only to hear his voice to vibrate to it like a musical instrument to a master hand.

Even with his eyes bandaged and under the doctor's strict instructions to stay in bed he was still his masculine, masterful self.

"Come here, my sweet," he said one evening when she had thought he was sleeping.

Quickly she had gone to his bedside.

"Do you want anything?"

"Yes!"

"What is it?"

He had reached up and pulled her down to him.

"Your lips, my darling!"

He had kissed her until her breath came quickly and her heart was beating suffocatingly in her breast.

"I love you!" Alec said hoarsely, "oh, God, how I love you and want you more than a man ever wanted a woman before!"

He had fought his way back to health and when finally the bandages were off and he could see, all he said was:

"You are lovely—even more lovely than I remembered!"

Now Vivian felt herself quiver because he was holding her and little thrills ran through her like the shooting stars she had seen when, almost on the point of collapse after a long day's march, she had led Alec to safety and civilization.

"Do you realize you are my wife—mine as I always knew you must be," Alec asked in a very deep voice.

"How could you have been so . . . sure?"

"We were meant for each other. It was fate—and I have

189

lived too long in the East not to know that when the wheel of life turns there is no escape."

"I thought . . . I hated . . . you," Vivian murmured.

"And now?" he asked.

She raised her face to his.

"I love darling Alec, I love you . . . desperately with . . . all of me! There is nothing else but . . . you!"

He pulled her closer and his lips were on hers holding her captive, making her feel that they were no longer two people but one.

He kissed her until the bungalow, the brilliance of the azaleas and the sunset disappeared. He kissed her eyes, her cheeks, her ears and the softness of her neck and again her mouth.

Then as the night came swiftly and suddenly it was dark, there was only the high note of a bat and the rustle of a small animal beneath them among the shrubs.

The stars were coming out one by one until the sky was brilliant with them, and Alec's lips grew more passionate, more demanding.

She felt him pull the pins from her hair, so that it fell over her shoulders.

He kissed it, and then as if its soft silkiness excited him, he swept it aside to kiss her neck again. He undid the back of her gown and his lips, fiercely demanding, were on the little hollow between her breasts.

Then gently but with an insistence that would not be denied, he drew her into the candlelit room behind them.

"My heart, my life, my soul," he said quietly, "for now and for all eternity!"

ON SALE WHEREVER PAPERBACKS ARE SOLD
— or use this coupon to order directly from the publisher.

BARBARA CARTLAND

V2705	**Again This Rapture** $1.25 £ (#36)
V3389	**Against The Stream** $1.25 £ (#68)
V2823	**Audacious Adventuress** $1.25 £ (#41)
V3491	**Coin Of Love** $1.25 £ (#3)
V2921	**Debt Of Honor** $1.25 £ (#16)
V3473	**Desire Of The Heart** $1.25 £ (#1)
V3271	**The Dream Within** $1.25 £ (#62)
V3537	**A Duel of Hearts** $1.25 £ (#8)
V2560	**Elizabethan Lover** $1.25 £ (#28)
V2769	**Enchanted Evil** $1.25 £ (#5)
V2795	**Enchanted Moment** $1.25 £ (#40)
V3048	**The Enchanted Waltz** $1.25 £ (#26)
V3019	**A Ghost In Monte Carlo** $1.25 £ (#48)
V3627	**Golden Gondola** $1.25 £
V3239	**A Halo For The Devil** $1.25 £ (#55)
V2706	**A Hazard of Hearts** $1.25 £ (#2)
V3358	**A Heart Is Broken** $1.25 £ (#66)
V2539	**Hidden Evil** $1.25 £ (#27)
V3538	**The Hidden Heart** $1.25 £ (#10)
V2636	**The Innocent Heiress** $1.25 £ (#15)
V3564	**An Innocent In Paris** $1.25 £ (#24)
V3326	**Josephine, Empress Of France** $1.25 £ (Biographical Romance)

Send to: PYRAMID PUBLICATIONS,
Dept. M.O., 9 Garden Street, Moonachie, N.J. 07074

NAME

ADDRESS

CITY

STATE   ZIP

I enclose $_____, which includes the total price of all books ordered plus 50¢ per book postage and handling for the first book and 25¢ for each additional. If my total order is $10.00 or more, I understand that Pyramid will pay all postage and handling.
No COD's or stamps. Please allow three to four weeks for delivery.
Prices subject to change.   P-15